SECRETS

Sequel to the best-seller, *SEASONS*

Also by Tina Melson

Seasons

A Christian Love Story

SECRETS

Sequel to the best-seller, SEASONS

Tina Melson

Books published by **The Butterfly Typeface Publishing** may be purchased for educational, business or sales promotional use. For information please write:

Attn: Iris M Williams, *The Butterfly Typeface Publishing*, PO Box 56193, Little Rock, AR 72215.

First Edition

ISBN: 978-1-947656-12-3

"I can do all things through Christ which strengthen me."

Philippians 4:13

Dedication

I dedicate this book to Abraham Harris because without his encouragement I would never have picked up my pen and finished this book. He encouraged me to dig deep inside myself, pull my dreams off the shelf and make them a reality.

Acknowledgments

I thank God first and foremost for allowing me to have the mindset and the patience to sit down and tell stories that can be heard. God gave me a vision many years ago and told me if I plant seeds they will grow.

I've planted so many seeds in the ground for this harvest. I've pulled up so many weeds that sometimes I thought I had sown on fallow/ hollow grounds!

Thanks be to God that some fell on good soil and my vision is beginning to grow. I give God all the praise!

He set me on a mission and without putting Latrea Wyche in my path, I never would have met Iris M. Williams and for these two beautiful angels, I give God the glory!

Tina Melson

Table of Contents

Foreword

Reading a Tina Melson book is an experience. The author weaves stories so real that you find yourself caring about her characters from the start and in fact, each of the characters could easily carry an entire storyline on their own.

The prayers she writes are straight from the author's heart and not only help the characters, but can help you the reader as well.

Many are of the false impression that being a Christian means being perfect, but Tina helps you to understand that often being a Christian means that you will come under attack faster and harder than the average person. She also helps the reader understand that while God didn't promise an attack-free life, He did promise to be there to help you through it.

In this life we will experience *Seasons* of abundance as well as lean times. We will do things for which we are not proud and that may cause us to live under a cloud of *Secrets*. What we have to remember is that there is nothing new

under the sun and therefore nothing too hard for
God to help us through.

Kudos to you Tina Melson for lending your talent
to the world and helping others understand that
God is with us always.

Iris M Williams

Author/Publisher

Preface

How could I end up in this situation? I've asked myself this question repeatedly over the course of the last few days. All I could think about now was how in the world was I going to come out of this? Why didn't I think before I acted? I remembered my mother's words now so many years after she had passed away, "You are going to get yourself in a world of trouble one day by thinking that the world owes you something. You had better learn to think with the right head that God gave you." She would say those words so often that I can still hear her voice as if she were standing right next to me. I have always thought that I was God's gift to women. Now that I've been hit with this information I'm not so sure. I am the head deacon of one of the biggest churches in Atlanta, and I am in for the fight of my life. I didn't intend for things to get so out of hand.

James didn't think to ask God for help because to him, it was always about what James wanted not about what he needed. Nevertheless, at this moment, he needed God.

Pacing around his spacious den, he looked out at the beauty of his yard and what he thought he had created all by himself. He was a very proud and private man. He began to pace again and to try to figure out just where he went wrong. He remembered feeling so excited that day. After he had gotten off work, he showered and took longer than usual to get dressed. He accessed his generous wardrobe, picked out one of his best suits, and pondered a few minutes about the color of his shirt and tie, but in the end, he chose a midnight blue shirt with a matching tie and was satisfied with his choice. As he backed out of his driveway, he looked in the rearview mirror at his big beautiful home and was puffed up with pride at all he had accomplished. Smiling to himself he gunned the motor to his new Jaguar and headed off for a night of fun and relaxation. He didn't know that God had a plan for his life.

Chapter 1- Seeing the Hidden Man of Darkness

"Let the church say Amen," Pastor G. Howard said to the congregation.

Everybody in the church said "Amen!"

Pastor Howard had taken over the church after Pastor Ron had retired two years prior. "Today is the day the Lord has made, and let us rejoice in it. There is a word from God. If you have your Bibles, turn to first Corinthians the second chapter verses five through nine."

As the Pastor was reading the scripture for that day's sermon, I peeked over at the second pew just to make sure she was still sitting there. She was! She was such a beautiful young woman with skin so honey brown and flawless. She really didn't need makeup; she had a nice body and big brown legs that made me want to... (Stop thinking about such things I reminded myself. You are a deacon, and you are in church!). I made myself come back to what Pastor was saying.

"Your faith should not stand in the wisdom of man but in the power of God. How many of us truly believe that God can do anything but fail? Are there any among us who, over the years, have heard this said by so many but only believe it because man said it, not because you have tried God for yourselves? I'm a living witness that God can do anything but fail. Sometimes God will let us go through trials and tribulations because He knows that unless you are tested, you will not come out as pure, or you won't come out at all."

People all around me were clapping and shouting. I always felt a little bit of envious of people when they were feeling God's presence in their spirit because I have truly never felt God's Spirit. Oh, I have felt good when my Pastor preached, but I have never felt it on the inside. Pastor Willis and I have had many conversations on this topic and more times than not, we have disagreed. I grew up in this neighborhood. Pastor Willis and I became good friends when we both worked together at Yamaha. Although he was years older than I, we formed a friendship that we've maintained all these years later.

He was the one to suggest that I become a deacon because of my faithfulness and dedication.   I was ordained years ago; now I was the chairman of the deacon board. As Pastor Howard was finishing his sermon, I heard him call out my name. For a minute, I didn't know what he wanted me to do; he was extending an invitation for anyone to join the church. After the service, Pastor Willis wanted to see me in his office.

"I just wanted to touch base with you James, just to make sure everything is all right with you." Pastor Howard was looking at me as if he could see through me.

"I've noticed that you don't seem to be yourself, and I wanted to know if there is anything I can do."

"Everything is fine." I answered hoping that this conversation wouldn't take long. "I've just got a lot going on in my life right now, and I'm trying to prioritize things. It's nothing I can't handle myself. I'm sorry if I seemed a bit out of sorts."

Pastor Howard looked at me for a minute and seemed satisfied with my answer. "All right, just so you know, I'm here if you need to talk." We shook hands, and I walked out of the office thanking God that our little talk was over.

As soon as I got home I changed into jeans, a polo shirt, and different shoes. Then I checked my messages. I saw that I missed the one call I had been expecting. I checked my messages to see if a message was left. As I looked in the refrigerator for something cool to drink, my phone rang.

"Hey," I went into my smooth talk phone voice. "I had a meeting after church. I just checked my messages, and I was fixing to call you back. Yes, we are still on; I'll be there in thirty minutes." I hung up and leaned against my counter top, drank the bottle water I was holding, and smiled. On my way out of the door, I looked in the mirror, hanging in the foyer, made sure I looked as good as I felt, and headed out.

"Today was going to be a day to remember," I thought to myself as I drove the rest of the way to Stone Mountain. I've been thinking about her all day! I didn't want to play games today; she knew that I was serious about what I wanted to do. I had been dining and buying her things for over two months, and today was payback for everything I had done. Don't get me wrong; I just feel like we are grown people, and grown people know what's up. I'm a man, and men have needs. I'm not into playing childish games. The first time I asked her out she said "No." It was like a slap in my face. I consider myself good looking, and I know any woman would be proud to just be with me. After she said no, I was determined to make her mine. The chase was a game to me, and I treated it as such. If I conquer her, she would pay dearly for turning me down the first time. Now the game was on. I had sent flowers to her job and to her home daily for two months, I took her out to dinner every weekend, and I even took her shopping twice. Maybe I did it because I liked my women to dress nicely and to compliment me.

I was a very secretive guy, and if it got out that I had dated and used so many women, I don't know what I would do. Well not really used in my mind because I gave good gifts and that should compensate for ridding me of those desperate women. I didn't think that anything was wrong with what I did. When it came down to it, I was all that mattered. Pulling into the drive, I cut the engine off and reached into the back seat for the bottle of wine and the flowers I had bought earlier. I had planned this evening out. I sat in the car looking at her home and the way she kept her grass cut and hedges trimmed.

I was impressed. I got out, walked up to the door, and rang the bell. She opened the door looking lovely as ever. The yellow sundress and small yellow and white sandals fit her small frame perfectly. Her hair was twisted up in a ball, and some curls were fanned out around her face. "You look lovely," I said.

"Come on in," she said turning away from me.

I pulled her into my arms and kissed those juicy lips. I couldn't help myself; I wanted to pick her up, carry her to the bedroom, and make love to her until I couldn't anymore, but I let her go. Stepping back, she led me into the den where she had laid out what looked to be a picnic on the floor.

"I hope you don't mind sitting on the floor; I've put out cushions all over, but we can move to the dining room if you like."

"No, I kind of like the idea of the floor. I brought you wine and some flowers."

She took the gifts and went into the kitchen. I looked around the room and saw paintings that were worth a lot of money. I couldn't deny that her furniture was top of the line. She had a surround system most people would die to have; walking around looking at the pictures on her wall, I wondered who this woman was? "Where did she work, and what kind of money did she have?" We never talked about our jobs or our families. Now I wondered why not. To be honest, I didn't want to talk about jobs or family; now I regretted not talking about those things.

Although her house was not as spacious as mine, everything was just as expensive and in place. She came back with the flowers in a vase, wine goblets, and a wine cork to open the wine. As we sat down to chicken salad that melted on your tongue, devil eggs to die for, and some other tasty exotic fruits, I wondered if she was the seducer and not me. I started to say something, but she interrupted me. "I've got something for you; wait here don't go anywhere."

She was out the door before a thought could form in my mind. A few seconds later she was back with an envelope in her hand; she handed it to me and said "Open it." I opened it, and much to my surprise it contained a check for everything I had done for her over the two months we had been together with interest. I looked at her and asked "What's this for"? Her response shocked me to the core.

She said, "When you first showed an interest in me, I was flattered. I thought you wanted what I wanted. Then you started dining me, sending me flowers, and buying me all sorts of things, but our conversations were never about us. You thought I needed you, and that's not the case. I needed us, but you showed no interest in getting to know me. You don't know what colors I like, what my favorite food is, where I work, or anything about me. So now I'm giving you back what you gave me with interest.

Who do you think I am?" She asked, "Do you think I'm one of those women that can't afford to take myself out to dinner, can't buy myself flowers, or clothing?"

I was shocked and really nothing came to my mind. She stood so I had no other choice but to stand as well.

I didn't know where this was going so I said, "Maybe I should leave." She just stared me down so I walked to the door, opened it, looked back, and said "I'll call you." I don't know who was mad at whom; all I knew was she was something serious, and I wanted to really get to know her better.

Shree wanted to talk to someone, but she didn't want the criticism she knew her best friend, Kim would give her. She decided to drop by GG's house. Shree had met GG twelve years ago, at Mt. Nebo. She was one of the first mothers of the church to welcome her. Although she wasn't Shree's birth grandmother, GG acted the part. Shree was grateful to have someone with such great wisdom with whom to talk. She grabbed her purse and headed to GG's house. There were several cars parked outside of GG's house when I arrived there. My first thought was something was wrong. I hopped out my car and almost twisted my ankle going to the door. Jackie, GG's granddaughter, answered the door, and I was surprised to see her.

"Hey, when did you get in town," I asked her giving her a big hug. Sherman had some loose ends to tie up so I came along to visit GG while he finished up; we were only here for the weekend.

Come on in and join us. Walking into GG's house was like walking back in time; she had so many memories from the past hanging on her walls. She also had pictures of famous people she had met over the years. We walked in the living room where Pastor Ron, his wife Christine, and GG were sitting, laughing, and talking.

GG looked up and motioned me over.

She gave me a big hug and said "I'm so glad you stopped by". Pastor Ron and Christine also gave me a hug.

"Sit down baby, Jackie was preparing dinner I hope you will join us. It's been so long since Pastor, Christine, and Jackie have been here. Now I feel like my whole family is here." I couldn't disappoint her so I accepted her offer.

My mind was racing in so many different directions, and it was getting harder to concentrate on what everybody was talking about. GG asked a question, and everybody looked at me.

I looked at GG and said to her" I'm sorry, what did you say?" She repeated the question without missing a beat,

"Are you feeling well dear?" "Oh yes, I'm fine."

At that moment, I knew that today was not a good day to have a talk with her. She was entertaining family and friends that she had not seen in almost a year; whatever was going on in my world would have to wait. I pulled it together and joined in the conversation.

Pastor Ron kept us laughing at all the things he and Mrs. Christine had been doing since his retirement from the church. After dinner and dessert, Pastor and Mrs. Christine excused themselves. Jackie and Sherman left to see the movie *War Room*. Everybody was talking about it. GG was looking a little tired so I told her that I would see her sometime during the middle of the week. GG looked me in the eye and said "It's not over until God says it's over."

I thought strange things were happening. I kissed her and headed home. In the car, I looked down at my phone and saw that I had ten missed calls. I decided to deal with them later because I was mentally exhausted. As I pulled into the driveway, James was sitting in his car like nothing had happened earlier.

"No!" Not tonight, I have nothing left to give anyone. I got out of the car, walked up to his door, and said, "Look, no more, I don't want to have a conversation with you tonight or any other night; go home or I will not be responsible for what is about to go down in my driveway." He took one look at my face, held his hands up, backed out the driveway, and kept going. I let out a sigh of relief and headed to my door. "Lord, how much more crazy stuff am I going to have to endure?"

Tina Melson

While unlocking the door, my cell vibrated. I looked down and saw that it was GG calling. I hit the end button, walked in the house, and started crying. What a mess of my life I was creating. I just couldn't talk to anyone right now. I knew that GG would call back. After taking a hot shower, I called her back, and before she could say anything, I apologized to her and told her that it had been a long day. GG let me off the hook but not until I promised her I would drop by after work tomorrow. I sat on my bed and started to wonder when my life had taken such a downward path.

James headed back home feeling angry and confused. No woman had ever treated him this way. Shree was not going to get away with it. The more he thought about it the angrier he became. After he pulled into the garage and got out of the car, he ripped his shirt off and went to the punching bag. He began to throw jabs as if it were a person. Blowing off steam helped him to feel a little better. His subconscious began to speak to him.

"What about prayer," it said. He didn't want to listen to reason; he just wanted revenge. "How could this woman dis me like that? Didn't she realize who I am? What I have? What I can do?" He was too upset for reason to enter his mind. The nerve of her giving the money back to him was too much for him to handle. The nerve of her not wanting him was making him go crazy. He wasn't being rational, and he didn't even care. He would just have to show her who he was, and with that thought, he began to feel much better.

He would give her just what she deserved! James knew that he was being irrational, but just thinking about getting even with her gave him the plan he needed to feel better about being dumped. Women just did not decline his gifts or his advances. He stepped into the shower and washed everything out of his mind except getting revenge on Miss Shree Wilson.

Shree on the other had was having a hard time dealing with the fact that she thought she needed a man to complete her. She worked hard at achieving all the goals she had written down so many years before.

Chapter 2 - Help, My Hurt is too heavy

The long drive from North Carolina to Atlanta left Shree and her parents tired and hungry. Her destination was Agnes Scott College. Her parents were so proud when the acceptance letter arrived. Although she had worked very hard during her four years of high school, Shree couldn't believe that she had been accepted. She wanted to make her parents proud. Her parents were hard working people. Every penny they saved went toward her college education. Gratefulness was a word that they lived by daily. On Sheree's last day home, her father came into her bedroom. With tear-filled eyes and joy in his heart, he said, "I'm so proud of you." Shree continued to reminisce.

I was having mixed emotions deciding what to pack when I heard someone knock at my bedroom door. I prayed it wasn't my mom because she had cornered me before my dad had gotten home from work and began that same song about the birds and bees, as though I didn't know about sex. I had seen what having sex could do to two people who really were not meant to be together. I was determined not to get caught up in the drama. My best friend, Mary, had started dating Demarcus in the ninth grade and had become pregnant during her senior year. Demarcus went to college, met another girl, and left Mary and the baby to take care of his new girlfriend and himself. Mary's mom had taken on the responsibility of raising baby Ayden so Mary could finish high school. I had lost touch with Mary because she joined the service so that she and Ayden could have a better life. We just started to lose touch with each other. I tried calling Mary to tell her about my college acceptance, but she never returned my call. Mom went on and on about everything until I wanted to scream! Finally, she allowed me to go up to my room and finish packing.

"Please don't let that be mom," I thought before I said come in.

Dad walked in my room looking a little down. "You got a minute Pumpkin?" That was the nickname he had given me; he called me that every chance he could. "I just wanted you to know how much I love you, how much I'm going to miss you, and how proud of you I am. We always wanted more than one child; I guess over the years it became less and less possible. I hope that I have been a good father to you and that I did what God commanded me to do by you. He said to train up a child in the way they should go, and when they are old they will not depart from it. I'm praying that you will always remember your upbringing and know that yes, you may make mistakes but try not to continue to make them.

What I'm trying to say is I know that things and people are going to approach you with all kinds of things, but remember that we, the Wilsons, serve an awesome God. Your mother and I tried to be good parents; we disciplined, admonished and counseled you. I only pray that our efforts were successful. I asked the Lord last night to give me a word for you, and now that He has, I just want to stand here, hug you, and not let you go. I know that it sounds foolish, but it feels as if I'm letting you go out to a world full of wolves without any protection. I stood there and watched the only man that I truly loved struggle to simply say he loved me. I threw my arms around his neck and cried.

"Look at us," he finally said crying like we would never see each other again. Finish packing and get some sleep because we leave at two in the morning.

My experience at Agnes Scott College was awesome; they taught me self-awareness. I learned who I was and what my passions were; I had opportunities to expand my awareness in life. I wanted to change and to make this world a better place. The first two years, I majored in nursing; I did the dual degree program. My minor was public health. During the first year, I met Debra. She was a tiny bit of a person. She was struggling in Spanish; I had learned it fluently. I offered to help her and we became fast friends. Debra was funny. She was also a daredevil, and we did all kinds of scary and fun things. Debra became like the sister I never had.

During spring break, Debra came home with me; my parents fell in love with her. Over Christmas break my parents came to Atlanta for two weeks. I had to stop myself from remembering any further because all my pain started on that day. I immediately began to cry earnestly; I cried for my mom, dad, Debra, but mostly for myself. I had no one, no one. A small voice inside of me said "You have me." It was a voice that I hadn't heard in a long time, but I ignored it. I heard it again saying, "The Lord is close to the broken hearted and saves those who are crushed in spirit." I was feeling so much pain at the core of my soul. I knew that God was talking to me; I just didn't know how to respond. He had taken everything I loved away from me, and I wasn't sure that I trusted Him anymore. I went back in time.

People were talking who I couldn't understand. I couldn't hear what they were saying. Someone started screaming and I was trying to see from where that terrible noise was coming. I saw Debra running down the hallway toward me. Then I saw darkness. That day my whole life changed. I couldn't think about it anymore; I had to get out of the house. I had to get some air. I grabbed my purse and keys headed for the car. For a moment, I thought, "Wait, where am I going? What was I doing?" I stood in the doorway crying as if it had just happened. My phone rang; I looked down at the caller ID. It was Kim. The only thing I said was,

"Just come over please; I'm ready to talk." I had run long enough, I was tired. Kim hung up and was there in fifteen minutes. We sat on the couch facing each other, and I began my journey back to the worst day of my life.

"My mom and dad should be here by now," I said to Debra riding back to the campus. We have so many plans, and I'm not sure we will be able to complete them all. It's been snowing all day.

Debra said, "Don't worry; your father knows how to drive in the snow."

Tina Melson
35

"I haven't talked to them in over two hours; I keep getting their voice mail."

"Your dad is probably taking his time," Debra assured me.

"Yeah, you're right," I said. As we got closer to the campus, I tried calling again. Still there was no answer; I said a silent prayer that they were okay. We were headed to our rooms when Mrs. Anthony, the school president, stopped us. "Can I speak with you privately Miss Wilson?

I whispered to Debra, "What have you done now?" She just shrugged her shoulders and smiled. I followed Mrs. Anthony to her office. When I stepped inside, there were at least half-dozen police officers, two of my professors, and the chaplain standing there. I started shaking, and my legs began to give way. Before anyone could say anything, I started screaming. Debra heard me and came running in shouting, "What happened! What is happening?"

She told me later that I had fainted. There had been a terrible accident on 285 right outside Atlanta; my parents didn't survive.

The next week was a nightmare. Debra's parents flew in from New York to help with the funeral arrangements. They did everything; I mean everything for me. I was in a fog during that time. My pastor came by, and what he said I couldn't even tell you because I don't remember. I do remember Debra and me just talking way into the night. Mostly Debra talked, and I just withdrew deeper and deeper within myself. Debra's father came to me on the evening before they returned to New York.

He said, "Baby, I know that this is tough for you, and I know that we won't always understand what God is doing in our lives, but you have to trust that He knows what He's doing. Don't get stuck in what you've been through. Otherwise, God can't take you where you're going. I know that you're hurting. You've had to bury both your parents. Let nothing separate you from the love of God. Try not to look at things from your natural eye but with your spiritual eye, and you'll see the goodness of God every time. Try not to be bitter. Your strength is made perfect in weakness. You will never know how strong you are until you see the strength of the attack against you. When something is opposing you, you will learn faith; either you trust God or not. Baby, continue to trust God.

Keep your hands in His hands, and He will see you through this.

I want you to call me if you need anything, and remember I love you." He kissed me on the cheek and hugged me as if I would never see him again.

After they left and I went back to school, I added more classes, aced all my tests, and worked harder than I had ever done before. I just wanted to honor my parents. I didn't go home with Debra during the summer. I just took more classes, and before I knew it, I was fluent in five languages:

Spanish, French, German, Japanese, and Chinese. Debra could hardly keep up with me.

By my third year, I had enrolled and had been accepted into Emory Woodruff's School of Nursing to complete my BSN. I told Debra that I was going to China during that next summer. She didn't want me to go; she wanted me to go home and spend the summer visiting her family. I went anyway, and while I was in China, Debra passed away. I started to cry again. Kim just rocked me in her arms like my mom used to do.

"Maybe you should try and get some sleep," Kim suggested. "I'll stay here tonight; we can talk more in the morning." I was exhausted.

I went upstairs, took a shower, and willed myself to stop thinking about the past.

The next morning, during breakfast, Shree looked at me and said, "I never knew Debra had Lupus. She never said anything, never showed fear, or pain. That summer I should have gone home with her. I could only see my pain, and I wanted to get away from everyone. The tears started to fall again. "No, no, I will not cry anymore," I said wiping my tears away.

"Do you think Debra forgave me?"

I looked at Shree in so much pain and said, "Yes, she forgave you. Now you just have to forgive yourself."

Tina Melson

Shree picked at her breakfast and said, "You know Kim, hurt people hurt the people that are closest to them. Maybe I was jealous that she still had her parents, and mine were dead. I don't know; I do know that I miss her. Debra was more than a friend; she was my sister."

"I know," Kim said. "Enough about the past, go get dressed for work. I'm going home to do the same, and I'll see you later this week."

We hugged, and Kim was gone. For some odd reason, Ephesians chapter 6 popped in my head, and I heard my dad saying, "Put on the whole armor of God, your battle has just begun." I had not spoken to God in a while. I prayed a prayer hoping God would hear it and forgive me. I left for work. Walking into her job, Shree was glad that during her last two years at Agnes Scott, she had been given the opportunity to intern at the CDC and Federal Reserve Bank of Atlanta. She did research trips to China, Germany, India, and Spain. Without those experiences, she would never have been able to head up the CDC here in Florida. She had written several books on Public Health Issues such as Anthropology, Sociology, Economics, and Women Studies. This job challenged her, supported her, and taught her how to take on the world. Everything was secure except her heart. Several times a day she thought about calling James, and every time the thought entered her mind, she pushed it aside. She knew that nothing was more deadly than self-righteousness, and he had a whole lot of that. He was so darn proud and arrogant, and she couldn't stand it. He didn't even know what kind of job she had, and he never asked. She went back down memory lane. He was so fine, skin smooth as a baby's bottom, and his smile, oh his smile, could stop traffic. Those pearly white perfect teeth, his juicy lips, and that banging body at his age, wait, she didn't even know his age. He had smiled at her, and she had melted right there, right there in the church. She was smitten with him.

When he walked up to her and asked her out, she almost fainted. All she could think about was their first date, the things she did with him, the way he made her feel, and the things he said that made her forget who she was and to whom she belonged. The secrets and the lies all led up to this moment, the moment of truth. Should she tell him or just pack up and run like she had all her life? She had to think about this carefully. She could destroy everything she had worked so hard to achieve. "Nowhere to run this time," a still voice in her heart said. What was she going to do? A knock at her door brought her back to the present.

My secretary stood at the door with papers I should have read earlier in the week.

"We have to get these documents signed and ready before the day's end Miss Wilson."

"Okay let's get to work." A terrible outbreak had happened and a press conference had been called at three that afternoon. I had to have accurate facts; lives were at stake. We finished just before three. I was so nervous when I stepped into the room of reporters waiting to take my statement. Acknowledging them I nodded that we were ready to begin. As you all are aware, a virus, that we've identified as Ebola, has broken out in Georgia and Florida. It is a disease that affects humans and other primates caused by Ebola viruses. The signs and symptoms typically start between two days and three weeks.

After contracting the virus, symptoms include: a sore throat, muscular pain, headaches, vomiting, diarrhea, and a rash. Those symptoms are usually followed by decreased function of the liver and kidneys. Sometimes people begin to bleed both internally and externally. This disease has a mortality rate killing between twenty-five and ninety percent of those infected. I have discovered that this is often due to low blood pressure from loss of fluids and typically follows six to sixteen days after symptoms appear. The virus spreads by direct contact with body fluids such as the blood of an infected person. Semen or breast milk of a person after recovery from EVD or Ebola might still carry the virus for several weeks to months. Blood samples are tested for viral RNA; viral antibodies of the virus itself confirm the diagnosis.

We must coordinate medical services alongside a certain level of community engagement. It needs to include rapid detection. Contact tracing of those who have come into contact with infected individuals, quick access to laboratory services, proper healthcare for those infected, and proper disposal of the dead through cremation or burial is urgent.

Samples of the body fluid and tissue from people with the disease should be handled with special caution. We must limit this outbreak ASAP. Protective clothing is a must, and washing hands is mandatory. Thank you all for your time.

Are there any questions?

Immediately everyone started asking questions. I had to let my press secretary calm everybody down just to get through the questioning. The last question was asked. "How many deaths have there been, and where is the biggest outbreak?"

After returning to the podium I said, "As of today September 27, 2015, this outbreak has had 2,424 reported cases resulting in 11,311 deaths. The largest outbreak thus far is in West Africa affecting Guinea and Sierra Leone. That's all I have for you today."

I walked away feeling as if I had the weight of the whole world on my shoulders.

Chapter 3 – Shhh, I've been Exposed

Pastor Ron was feeling restless that morning. He told Christine that he was going to take a drive and get some fresh air. He had tossed and turned most of the night. He knew what he needed to do, and now he was on a mission to take care of business. As he pulled into the parking lot of James's law firm, he sat for a minute talking to God. Once he was satisfied with what he was going to say to James, he got out of the car and walked up to the door. The doorman greeted him. He looked around admiring the vastness of the place and headed to the bank of elevators that would take him to James's office. Stepping off the elevator onto the fifteenth floor, he was amazed at the décor in the lobby. "This is truly fit for a king," he said to himself. Mrs. Pittman, James's head secretary, looked up as the elevator door closed.

"Good morning Pastor Ron, how are you? I didn't see you on Mr. Favors's calendar this morning."

"No, I just stopped in this morning hoping to get a chance to talk to him and catch up on a few things."

"Let me see if he's available."

She stepped out from behind her desk and disappeared through a door I had not noticed before. Several minutes passed before she came back and announced,

"Mr. Favors will see you now."

I was led into an office the size of a small house. James was getting up and walking toward me with is hands outstretched. 'Pastor," he said as we both hugged each other. "How's it going? When did you get back in town? Why haven't you called me?"

He had so many questions for me. "Let's sit and chat if you have time."

"Oh, I'll make time for you, Pastor Ron.

Mrs. Pittman hold all my calls and get us coffee please." After she left, we grinned at each other and said, "Always together Ron and James," which had us laughing like school boys. "What really brought you downtown Ron?

"You know we got back in town on Sunday and had dinner with GG. I came by today to have a serious talk with you. You know you're my friend and I have your back!"

"Yeah, I know, but you're sounding serious like you know something I don't know. What's going on?

Is there something you wanna tell me, or should I just tell you what I suspect?"

"I don't know what you're talking about." Ron just sat there looking at me as though I was lying. Finally, he shook his head and said, "Come on James, it's just you and me talking friend to friend."

Tina Melson
44

"Okay Ron, I'll come clean," I said all the while thinking that I never could put anything pass him except "My secret affairs," my inner voice said. "Look man, do you remember that fine lady that came to the church about twelve years ago? The one you said was broken and God was putting her back together again?"

"Yeah, you mean Shree?"

"Yea that's her. I started to notice her over time. She was always sneaking a peek at a brother, and I just had to have her. I asked her out a few times and bought her some expensive gifts. One thing led to another, and you can figure out the rest. Last weekend after church, I went to collect on some of those gifts, but things didn't work out like I planned."

"How so?"

"We were at her house; soft music was playing. She had fixed a picnic in the middle of her den. I had gotten comfortable. She left the room. I was thinking she would slip into something more comfortable. She returned with the same clothes on and an envelope, which she handed to me. Her whole attitude had changed, and she began to tell me that she knew me for who I was and that I never had her best interest at heart. She said all I wanted was sex, and I didn't even know her favorite colors or what her favorite dish was. She went in hard on a brother, and to top it off, she gave me everything back that I had given her plus interest.

Man, I was shocked that she had the nerve to do that to me! I had looked around, and I knew that she had some things going on because her home had some very expensive stuff in it. Plus, she drove a very nice car. I never thought she was balling like that. She threw me out."

Ron started laughing so hard that I got upset all over again. When he finished laughing he said, "That explains why she was so pre-occupied when she got to GG's house. She couldn't keep up with the conversation we were having."

"Man, I'm so angry with her." "This is why I came down here to have a talk with you. Last night I had you on my mind so heavy. You have to know that you cannot hurt, harm, or endanger this woman. She belongs to God."

"What? Man, what you talking about?" "Look, you were called to love this woman and to love her unconditionally. Don't look at things through your natural eyes but through your spiritual eyes. See you're trying to pay back someone for something you did. She didn't hurt you; you hurt you."

"What? I'm not following you." "Listen, you chased her in your mind before you ever asked her out. She saw the God in you before she said yes. Your intentions were wrong. As long as you have been a deacon in the church, I have been praying that God would change your ways and actions. Look, I know what you have been up to, and I have been praying that God would help you. You have declared war on yourself, and now you have to repent and sincerely change your ways. I see you trying to repay evil for evil, but revenge belongs to God alone. She hasn't done anything but try to love you."

"Wait a minute; are you saying she talked to you about me Sunday?"

"No, I'm saying God talked to me about you. Don't touch His anointed." "Now that's funny because she did everything she could to make me her man. What I'm telling you is she's not the little church girl you think she is."

"I'm not here to get into what she is and what she's not. I'm here because I've been your friend forever. I'm here to tell you to repent and to change your ways. God is in full control and what you are doing and have done stinks to Heaven."

"Oh, you come into my place of business telling me to change like you've been righteous all your life!"

By now, James was furious and nothing the good Reverend could say would calm him down.

"I think I'd better go until you've calmed down."

"Yeah, I think you should."

We were facing each other as though we were getting ready to brawl so I turned around and walked out. I was like a raging bull in a China shop after Ron left.

I grabbed my jacket and headed down the back elevator to my car. I wanted to punch someone; no, I wanted to kill someone. I sat inside my car and replayed the conversation which upset me even more. I envisioned myself pulling up to Shree's job and choking her to death. I know she talked about me to everyone who would listen. She had to pay; she just had to because my reputation was on the line. I just needed to come up with a plan. A still small voice in the back of my head was telling me to stop and think, but I wouldn't listen. I pulled out of the garage and headed west on Route 66. I had no idea where I was headed, but I drove through traffic thinking about what I wanted to do.

Pastor Ron sat in his car trying to figure out where the conversation between James and himself went wrong. He never thought it would get out of hand. They had always been able to talk about anything. God, I thought this would be easy. I thought his mind would be open to reason. He just could not believe the person he just talked to was his friend. Something was terribly wrong with James. He was not the same person I had known. Lord, I just don't know what to do so I'm asking for your guidance in this matter. "Touch James's mind; touch his heart. Lord, touch his life." I prayed all the way home. Christine was sitting on the porch when I arrived. After getting out the car, she met me with a kiss and a hug. I hugged her back and said, "You are the best thing that has ever happened to me. Do you know how much I love you?"

She responded with another kiss and a smile. "Where have you been? You looked so stressed when you pulled up? What in the world have you been up to?"

"Come on, let's go into the kitchen, and you can fix me lunch while I tell you."

I began to tell Christine about my conversation with James and about the way he acted toward me. Christine was not at all surprised. "Honey, you were so blind as to how proud and arrogant James was. Even when you were the pastor at Mt. Nebo, you couldn't see him for who he was. I knew this day would come; now, you must pray and ask God for His guidance in this matter. Nevertheless, I think we should pray for him together." We joined hands and bowed down right where we were. My husband went to God in prayer ...

"Most Gracious and Merciful God, we come to say thank You for Your continuous love You have for us. Thank You Lord for Your anointing on our lives as we offer up intercessory prayer for our dear brother James. Lord, we know that our ways are not Your ways nor our thoughts higher than Yours. As we are working on the outside appearance, You are already working on the inside for our good. Lord, I don't know what James has in his mind to do, but we ask that You intercede on his behalf; regulate is mind. Lord, create in him a clean heart and renew the right spirit within him. Lord, we know that You and only You can change mindsets. You are the Great I Am, and for this, we give You honor and glory.

My brother James needs You right now Lord. Strengthen him where he's weak, and build him up where he's torn down. Lord, let him resist the devil. Your Word tells us that the Devil shall flee, and right now, we bind up the Devil in James's life. We cast him back into the pits of Hell where he belongs. Wash James thoroughly from his iniquity and cleanse him from his sins. Let him hear the joy and gladness that You promise in Your Word. Deliver James from evil, and bring him back into Your good pleasures. Hear our cry O God; attend unto our prayer. Hide him under the shadows of your wings. This prayer we pray in the Mighty Name of Jesus Christ, and it is so done. Amen, Amen, and Amen."

Tina Melson

After praying, Pastor Ron went to his study to talk to God alone. Christine knew that it was left in God's hand and that Ron needed time by himself. She began preparing lunch so that when Pastor was finished they could sit down and eat. She was so busy in her thoughts. She didn't hear the doorbell ring the first time. Someone knocked on the kitchen door. Christine looked around and saw Nicki standing at the door. "Child, I was so deep in thought I didn't hear you. Come on in, and have a seat. I just made fresh lemonade; let me get you a glass."

Nicki said, "If this is a bad time, I'll come back."

"No, Ron and I were just about to eat lunch so your timing is perfect; join us please. Where is my grandbaby?"

"She's with Gregg in the park, so I decided I would stop by and talk to you and pastor."

Nicki needed her mother's advice on how to handle a problem at the church. Pastor Ron walked into the kitchen and said, "What a wonderful surprise! I didn't know you were coming to lunch."

"I didn't either, but since I was invited to stay, I need to talk to both of you about James."

After Pastor said grace, Nicki started to share what was on her mind. "Being first lady of a church is not an easy job. Women come to you with secrets and want advice on all sorts of things. To be honest, I just don't know what to tell them at times, which brings me to James. He seems to be the center of attention for most of these women. I do not understand is how he has time to date so many women. It began two years ago when Mrs. Stephen's daughter, Rebecca, came by my office after church. She wanted to talk to Pastor Howard about James and how James was treating her. Gregg and I thought James was finally ready to settle down. Gregg had a talk with him, and James swore that Rebecca was stalking him. Gregg believed him. I sat down with Rebecca and had a long talk with her. She swore that they were having an affair. Gregg and I set up a conference with both of them. She never showed up; in fact, she never came back to church. After talking with Mrs. Stephens, we found out Rebecca had moved away.

At the time, we thought that that was such a strange thing for her to do. Less than a month later, Chundra, the choir director, came to me about James. She told me that she was dating him, and it looked like they would be getting married soon. That didn't work out, and I've noticed a big change in Chundra since. She's not the same energetic person she used to be. Then Mary Ann, the best singer we have, came to me wanting advice on abortion. You know how we feel about that. Therefore, I started a single's ministry at the church. I had to implement something for these women. I've pleaded with Gregg to talk with James or sit him down, but Gregg won't talk about this with me. Moreover, I heard from Jackie that Amanda lost her husband and child because she was seeing James as well. These women have all had something to do with James in one way or another, and he continues to sit on the board of deacons. He looks all proud and puffed up like nothing can touch him. I need some advice." We looked at each other, and Ron cleared his throat. He told Nicki that he would talk to Pastor Gregg and see what could be done. Nicki seemed relieved. We finished lunch, and she left. I came back into the kitchen, looked at my husband, and said, "You know you cannot talk to Pastor Gregg about James.

" He looked at me, and said, "I know, but I can't stand by and watch James destroy himself. You know we are our brother's keeper."

James was still furious. He drove to Shree's job and sat outside waiting for her to come out. A security guard drove by, parked in front of him, got out of his vehicle, and walked up to the window to see if he could be of assistance.

"Are you waiting on someone he asked James?"

James looked up at him, and said, "No, I'm trying to find the Federal building, but I think I made a wrong turn." The guard gave him directions. James thanked him and drove off. "What am I thinking," he thought to himself "I need to go home and rethink this situation?"

He got back on the interstate and drove home. Once he was home, he headed upstairs to take a shower and clear his head. An hour later, he was dressed and ready to contemplate his next move. He knew that time was of the essence.

Thinking back, he remembered the narrow escape he had with Rebecca. He had seduced her and paid her off. He even went as far as to secure a job for her in Chicago. That was a costly situation. Even to this day he had to send monthly payments to her. Then there was Chundra, but she was a weak little thing. She was easy to keep quiet; Mary Ann, on the other hand, was tricky because she thought she was carrying his child, and he had to convince her that he could not have children due to injuries he sustained as a teenager. He had stopped chasing women for a while until he saw how Shree looked at him when she thought he wasn't looking. Now she could ruin him, and all he had worked so hard for.

How had things gotten out of hand so quickly? He knew she had the power that no other woman had and that was the power to possess his heart. He couldn't pay her off; she had just as much as he did or even more. Did he really want to hurt her, or did she want to hurt him? Thinking back, it was him who pursued her not her who pursued him. He had finally met his match. Darn, he was thinking too hard. Maybe a drink was what he needed. Yeah, he'd get up, pour himself a drink, relax his body, and clear his mind.

He had heard his mom say, "Lust always gives out; but love lasts forever."

He had lusted after so many women, and now he was tired. He had always prided himself in keeping it together when things were falling apart. He still wanted Shree, and everything in him told him he did. Now she had gone and messed things up for him. He had to come up with a plan. His phone rang, and looking down. he saw that his pastor was calling. "Lord, give me strength." he thought before he answered.

"Pastor how you doing? Is everything alright," James asked.

"The board is meeting tonight, and I was checking to see if you were going to be there. I know that you were in litigation with a big case this week."

"Yes, I finished a little early today. I'll be there on time."

"Fine we'll see you around seven."

"I'll be there." I hung up and prayed that I wouldn't look like I felt when I walked inside the church tonight. The choir was finishing the song "Fill Me up Lord."

I walked through the door and stood there listening to them sing the lyrics. "If You provide the fire..." I almost lost it standing there listening to the words I had to walk away and wipe my eyes. My mom had not raised me this way; that song touched every fiber of my being. She used to tell me that temptation can only occur when you want something, not God but you. She told me it would be Satan. She said, "You have the ability to call forth life not death." "Lord, what had I done?"

I went into the restroom and cleaned myself up before anyone could see me crying like a baby. I wanted to fall down and beg for God's forgiveness, but I had too much pride. I couldn't bring myself to do it, not now and not here. I walked out and ran right into Pastor Gregg. "Brother James, I was looking for you. Is everything alright?"

"Yes Pastor, I'm fine." "I thought I heard someone crying in there."

I looked back toward the bathroom and asked, "Where in the men restroom?"

"Yes," Pastor Gregg said, "As a matter of fact, I was headed in to see if I could help."

"There is no one else in there. Just me, and I certainly wasn't crying. What you heard was me trying to sing." We both laughed, and he patted me on the back. We headed to the meeting.

The meeting lasted longer than I thought, and I was ready to leave when Pastor Gregg said, "Hold up a minute Deacon. I need to talk to you in private." After the others left, we sat facing each other. He said, "I didn't want to bring up this matter tonight, but it seems that I have no other choice. Rumor has it that you're seeing one of our members, and things are not going well. I don't like getting into private matters, but if it will affect the church, I think you and I need to talk about it."

"Pastor, it's like you said 'Rumor has it.' I'm not dating anyone here, and whatever you've heard is just a rumor."

"I have no other choice, but to believe you James. I'll just put the matter to rest for now."

He stood and patted me on the back. We walked out of the church together. While getting in my car a voice said, "Why you didn't talk to him?"

"I didn't know how," I said to myself. I drove home thinking about how I could have solved this problem if I didn't have so much pride. I could have been honest with Pastor Gregg for once in my life and could have gotten so many things off my chest. When I was twenty-two and fresh out of college, my mom said that my head was bigger than my heart. I wanted to chase women like my daddy did, and in doing so, he had torn our family apart. I was smart or so I thought. Why marry when you can have as many women as you like? Nobody would be the wiser. I would work hard all week and save my money for the finer things in life. I knew that women loved to be with men that had big things like homes, cars, and businesses. I was determined to have the best things that money could buy.

I always went to church because that's how my mama raised me. She used to say, "James, hearing the Word of God will not heal you; doing what the Word says will." Now all these years later those words have come back to haunt me. I didn't have many friends because I never wanted anyone to see my flaws.

I kept to myself. My mom knew God, and she would say, "Your sins will find you out one day. You have got to have faith in God not in James. James will fail you, but God will never leave or forsake you. James, why don't you just be a positive influence in people's lives? Everybody has a heart some harder than others but a heart nevertheless. God didn't make men to hurt each other but to love unconditionally." My mom was a great lady of wisdom, and now, I missed her more than anything. When she died five years ago, GG tried to take her place in my life, and I rejected her.

 She still said, "If you ever need to talk to someone close to God, I'll be here. God see's everything, and I feel your pain." I thought she was being nosy. I chose to stay away from her; now, I wished that I had gotten closer to her. I could surely use a good friend now. Maybe I would swallow my pride and call Pastor Ron; he has always been there for me. I know what I did the other day was uncalled for, but I had felt as though my back was against a wall. I had lashed out. I really needed to talk to someone. I picked the phone up and called Pastor Ron.

Chapter 4 – Face-Off with Myself

GG had driven herself over to Shree's house; GG felt the need to have a one on one chat with her. After parking in the driveway, GG looked around at the beautiful flowers in the yard, the well-cut grass, and the shrubbery surrounding Shree's property. She felt her heart swell with pride. She was always proud when she could see God's hand in people's lives. However, something wasn't setting right with her concerning that girl, Shree had changed, and the change had come a few weeks ago. GG was there to find out what it was. She got out of the car and walked up the steps of this grand home. It was cumbersome, but she knew that God wouldn't take her before her time. GG was out of breath by the time she rang the doorbell. She waited for the door to open. She knew that Shree was in there lurking behind the curtains. GG had seen them moving as she approached. Shree opened the door and ushered GG inside.

"Have a seat, and I will be right back. I had just put on tea."

GG sat down and looked around the beautiful room. She thought that this room should be filled with children. Shree came back with a pot of tea and two cups. "I don't know what made me fix tea today, but I suddenly had a taste for it. After pouring tea into both cups, she looked up at GG and said, "So GG what brings you all the way out here?"

GG replied, "I wanted to sit down and talk to you without interruption. I knew I had to come here. You have done well for yourself; you do know this. You have a beautiful home with nice furnishings, and yet, you are lonely. Tell me what you are looking for."

This was the GG she knew, always straight to the point. Shree started crying and GG said, "No dear, now is not the time for tears. Tell me what you are looking for." I dried my eyes and looked into GG's face.

"I messed up this time; I messed up big. I don't know what I was thinking. My flesh got in the way of my dreams. I was taught better, and I knew better." I knew the only way to keep GG's trust was to tell the truth, and that's what I was doing.

"I started dating this guy. I thought he was looking for the same thing I was looking for. In the beginning, everything was fine. Then, I started to notice things like he didn't know my favorite color, foods I like, or flowers I like. He didn't even know where I worked, or what I did for a living. His interest was my body, and I wasn't concerned at the time. However, now I'm in trouble, and I'm very concerned. I was in a secret relationship, and it has affected my entire life."

"God is ready to forgive you Shree, but you have to first forgive yourself."

GG took my hand and said, "Nothing is too hard for God. Do you believe that?" I couldn't answer her. "Baby, God is calling you to a higher place of intimacy in Him. Let go of whatever is keeping you bound and out of His presence. Nothing is worth your relationship with God."

I looked at GG with tears in my eyes and said, "Not even the child I'm now carrying?"

GG replied, "Nobody is perfect child, not even me. I know that you think this is the worst thing that has ever happened to you, but it's not. You think that you made a mistake, but you didn't. Sometimes we move ahead of God. It's not that we aren't going to have what we desire; God just simply says, 'Not right now.' You moved ahead of God. Now you have to stand right here, and watch God work things in your favor. It's not our timing but God's. I was just thinking that this room should be full of children. Although your method in filling it was not right, it's already done. We can only pray that blessings will come from it. Who is the young man that you didn't talk to God about?"

"James."

"I thought as much. He has a good heart, but pride is a problem.

I have been praying for him and planting seeds in him a long time. I only hope that he chooses whom he will serve. I pray that the God in him is bigger than the Devil in him. He's fighting for his life now, and there is nothing you or I can do but pray. I tried to be there for him when his mother died a few years back, but he wanted to be left alone. I prayed for him then, and I'm praying for him now." "Tell me about the grandmother of my child GG."

"Well, she was a beautiful woman, well dressed and highly favored by God. She could have easily been a pastor. God had given her a lot of wisdom and knowledge. She kept a firm hand on James. He was always a handful. She was smart and funny. She married James's father after high school, and we all thought things were fine. James's dad, Deion, was a football star; he even played pro ball for a few years until he blew out his knee. James is a lot like Deion; as far as women are concerned, he loved them. Maria knew all of this going on and it didn't seem to bother her because she thought she could change him. She couldn't, and she stayed with him until James was in his second year of college.

I don't think she divorced him. I think she just left him. He didn't know that he was going to miss her so much. After she had been gone for a year, he started drinking and ended up with liver cancer. He died about two years before she died. James buried his grief in working and getting degree after degree.

That's how he got that big law firm. He built his mama that big beautiful house he lives in, and she never got to live in it. After that he and Pastor Ron became the best of friends. I thought James was going to be okay. I'm not saying that he's not doing well; I'm just saying that too much too soon can sometimes cause a person to act out of character. He's reached an age in which most men should be settled down and enjoying the fruits of their labor not running wild. I want you to know that God's mercy is bigger than any mistakes that you've made.

He is here to forgive you; all you have to do is ask. Have you told him that he's going to be a father?"

"No, because after I found out that he wasn't interested in being in a monogamous relationship, I gave him a check for everything he had ever given me and put him out of my home. He's angry, and I am too."

GG insisted, "Don't you think it's time that you two sit down and have a talk?"

"Maybe, I don't want him to think that I trapped him into being a father."

GG looked at her and shook her head. "The mistake was made when you decided to have sex before marriage, and now you both have to take responsibility for this child that's growing inside of you. I'm leaving now, and I want you to call him and tell him."

"I'm scared GG; I don't know how he's going to react."

"Shree, it doesn't matter if he accepts or rejects you. You are going to be that child's mother, and he will be the father. Don't delay; tell him."

I walked GG to the door and watched her make her way to her car and drive off. I sat down in the chair where GG had sat earlier and cried until I had no more tears. I must have fallen asleep because when I woke up the house was dark just like my life. I was hungry so I went into the kitchen to fix something to eat. I munched on an apple while I waited for my frozen dinner to cook. I tried to see where my life was headed. I didn't want to bring a child into this world without a father. I didn't want to be a single mother. I was careless, and it was nobody's fault but mine. I walked outside of God's will for my life. I didn't take the time to ask God if James was the man for me. I wanted what I wanted with no thought of the consequences it would bring. I wanted to tell James that I was carrying his child, but I also didn't want him to know. I could transfer to Atlanta, but that wouldn't be fair to the child that I was now carrying.

Would he think that I set a trap for him?

Would he be happy?

Would he be angry? I just didn't know.

I did know that it was ten o'clock at night, and I was hungry. I ate the frozen dinner and looked in the pantry. I found some cookies and almost ate the entire bag.

Although I was still hungry, I went upstairs, took a shower, and got in bed. I turned the TV on and flipped through the channels looking for anything to take my mind off of James. Nothing was on so I grabbed my mother's Bible. I found peace in Psalms 23. I had known God when I was growing up, but I had strayed when my parents died. Sometimes when trouble comes you just don't know how to handle it. Sometimes you do things that are not pleasing to God. I was in college, and I wasn't what you would call a bad girl. I didn't go to church.

The things in the world looked good and felt good. I had no one but Debra. I had met her that first year of college. After my parents had passed, Debra's parents tried to be there for me, but I needed to get away. I signed up for the college tours that took me all over the world. My studies were the only thing on my mind. After graduating from college, I met Steve, and that's when I got wild. Steve was everything and nothing a girl needed. He could have helped me ruin my life, but there was some good in him. After living with him for a year, he told me that he would buy me a one way ticket to anywhere in the world. He actually saved my life! I choose Miami. He put me on a plane to Florida with five thousand dollars and a prayer. I tried to find him to thank him, but I couldn't. I hadn't thought about Steve in years. I wonder what happened to him. Tomorrow I'm going to look on the internet and see if I can find him. I made that promise as I closed my eyes and sleep overcame me.

James was headed out the door when Pastor Ron pulled into his driveway.

James groaned, "What now."

He put a smile on his face and walked outside to greet his friend.

"Hey, what brings you by," James asked. "

I got your message, and I thought I would drop by and have a little chat." James had forgotten that he had called him earlier. "You want to come in or would you rather sit out here."

"We can talk inside." I turned, unlocked the door, and walked inside with Pastor Ron on my heel. He moved around me and sat down in my favorite chair. He had the the biggest grin on his face.

"Alright," I told him. "Point taken. I'm going to be the bigger man and apologize to you for what happened the other day. I'm sorry that things got out of hand."

Ron just nodded his head. "Well," I said looking at him. "Oh, you waiting on me to apologize," he said.

"I was hoping you would."

"Okay James, I apologize." He stood up and gave me a bear hug. "What's on your mind he asked sitting back down?"

I hesitated for a moment. Then I decided that I needed to get some things off my chest. "You ordained me as a deacon, and I think you knew I wasn't ready at that time. I was still out there. Since that time, I have been running farther and farther away from God. I've done so many women wrong, and it's finally catching up with me. I don't know where to begin building my life back. Tonight I walked in the church, and the choir was practicing. They were singing this song called *Fill Me Up*. It took me by surprise, and my knees literally buckled under me. Every woman I had done wrong popped into my memory. I need to make it right by them. I need to ask for their forgiveness. I prayed like I never had before. To think that I am the very thing that disgusts me in other men, I am that man. I have become my father." Pastor Ron sat silently listening to James talk before he spoke. "My mom use to say, 'There is a day coming that will bring men's secret sins into the open.' I guess today is my day.

All that we are, all that we do, and all that we have are due to the free and rich grace of God so no man has reason to be proud. I have been a proud man, and for that, I'm sorry. I'm so sorry."

Pastor Ron patted James on the back and said, "Don't get stuck in what you've been through. Otherwise, God can't take you where you need to be. I ordained you because I knew what was inside of you. If I had not stepped in you would have destroyed yourself. God called you a long time ago, but you were not listening.

You had to get to this moment for you to see that this is not who you are. Now you are hungering and thirsting after righteousness, and God is ready to fill you up. Years ago, I heard a pastor say that God allows trouble to go on for years just to set the stage so that when He delivers you, you will know that it was nobody but God. He is pushing you into your purpose. All this time you have been looking for something in a dead place. You have been set free this day. You have been sowing seeds on hard ground. Now it's time to sow on good ground. Get rid of hatred in your heart; get rid of envy and jealousy. You are about to go through your greatest battle, but recognize God in the mist of it. God is calling you to a higher place of anointing in Him. Let go of whatever is keeping you bound and out of His presence. Nothing is worth your relationship with God. Repent and let it go."

Chapter 5 – Mr. Fix it

Pastor Ron got in his car and let out a big glory hallelujah to God. He thought that his talk with James was the beginning of change that he so desperately needed. Pastor Ron knew that all had sinned and God did give second even third chances. He smiled as he backed out James driveway.

James stood looking out the window thinking hard about what he was about to do. He had to begin to fix his life if he stood any chance of redemption. James looked at the clock, it was nine, he thought he would start with Rebecca she was always up late he recalled. He dialed her number waiting for her pick up. Rebecca had just come in from a long day at work when her cell rang. She looked at the caller ID and saw James number and decided to not answer.

Rebecca was getting home sick. She missed her family especially her mom. Greed can make even the best people seem like the worst people. She started thinking about how she had let James manipulate her into coming to Chicago for a fresh start. He had arranged for her to work in his partner law firm and at first the ideal sounded too good to be true.

 He had convinced Rebecca that wither skills and degree she would make partner in less than a year.

The winters were brutal and the litigations were endless all she had accomplished was lead litigator. She had worked tireless on so many cases that she thought she would never litigate again. She hated her job but most of all she hated James. His friend Jim Davis was not only a tough boss but he seemed not to care for people at all. The pay was good but not as good as it should have been. She hated Chicago. All her hard-earned money went to pay bills or was sent home to help her mom out. The more she thought about James the more she wanted to ruin him. She had let a man separate her from God and her family. Church was not an option here.

She worked twelve-hour days six days a week and on the seventh day she just wanted to rest. She had not found a church and didn't have the energy to look for one she just wanted to go home. Rebecca had thought that she loved James; he had promised her that he would one day marry her and like a fool she had believed him. He hadn't been to Chicago once in the almost two years she had been there. As she thought back on the reason she was there it was all about getting her out of his life. He never loved her he had used her like all the others she had heard rumors about. The more she thought about it the angrier she got. He had put up a good point talking about how Florida had nothing for me there. How I can make a fresh start in Chicago and he would follow me when he sold his business.

I must have been a fool to believe him no I was a fool. The winters were like none I had ever known. I hated the snow and the fact that nothing ever closed down; you just keep pressing your way through. I wanted to go home but I knew that I couldn't take care of my mom on the salary I made in Florida the way I was taking care of her now. I thought about her growing older and me not being there to take care of her and I began to cry. I just wanted to go home. Realizing that I was thousands of miles away my heart broke in a thousand pieces as I cried. Looking at my phone and the message light blinking I pushed the button to hear another one of his lies.

Rebecca this is James I'm flying into Chicago in the morning on business and I was hoping we could do lunch or an early dinner we need to talk, I'll call you as soon as I touch down. I listened to his message four times to make sure he said that he was coming. I wondered if he was coming to propose to me or if he was still playing games. I wouldn't let myself get excited I had not seen James since I left Florida. I knew in my heart that he didn't love me so I refused to get my hopes up. I would not call him back but I looked forward to his visit. I felt the sudden urge to pray so I got on my knees right where I was and prayed...

Lord I know it's been a long time since you've heard from me and I'm sorry. I'm so sorry that I have done thing's that's not pleasing to you. I know that your word tells me that you are a God of second chances and I'm asking for a second chance. A chance to get my life back on track, Lord, you are my fortress my place of safety and I trust you. In Psalm ninety-one you said I have no need to worry about the dangers by night or the arrows during the day so I give every weight that so easily get to me over to you. I love you Lord and I repent of all the wrong I've done. I ask that you order my steps from this moment on, in the mighty name of Jesus Christ, Amen and thank God.

With tears streaming down my face I got up and started to praise God, something I hadn't done in almost two years. I felt like a new person. After taking a shower I got my Bible out and read all of Psalm 91 and Psalm 23. I knew that God was going to see me through this and I fell asleep.

My alarm went off right at six and I got up went into the kitchen made a cup of coffee and opened the Bible up to Psalm 23 said a quick prayer. The shower felt so good I didn't want to get out. After dressing I left for work. On the drive downtown I couldn't wait to get to work and see if Jim knew that his partner was flying in this morning. Two peas in a pod were all I could think of to call them this morning. Walking into the office I saw Jim up ahead of me and I hurried to catch up with him.

Good morning, I said walking beside him.

Well good morning Rebecca you're in a good mood.

Yes don't you want to know why? I got a call last night from James he's coming to Chicago this morning.

Jim stopped walking and looked at me. He's what? Yes he's coming today.

Jim ushered me into his office and closed the door. Did he say why? He didn't call me. No all he said was he would be here today. Jim looked nervous and I laughed.

Why the long face won't you be happy to see him? He hasn't been here in over a year.

Did you call him Jim asked me looking at me suspicious?

No he called me. Aren't you happy about him coming? He stammered while trying to answer me.

Yeah, yeah I just wished he would have given me a heads up that's all. Jim's secretary interrupted our conversation by announcing that Mr. Favors was waiting to see him. Shall I show him in? He looked like we had gotten caught with our hand in the cookie jar. I didn't understand his reluctant in seeing James. Do you want me to leave I asked him.

No, you stay right here. Show him in Mrs. Connor please. James walked in and saw me standing beside Jim came over and gave me a hug shook Jim's hand and said did I miss a meeting or something?

Jim laughed nervously and I just shrugged my shoulders. so you two look like I interrupted a meeting or something. Oh he was smooth I thought to myself. No I was briefing Rebecca for today's litigations. Maybe I should wait outside he said smoothly. No we are finished. He looked at me, well if I can have a few minutes of your time Jim I would like to go over something with you. That was my hint to leave so I excused myself and walked to the door but before I could open it James said if it is possible Rebecca I'd like to take you to lunch.

I turned and said I'd like that and walked out the door. Shutting my office door I sank into my chair and laid my head on my desk. Just seeing James made me want to do crazy things. I had to pull myself together. He was so fine. I got dizzy just looking at him. I wondered what brought him here. I would soon find out. Pulling myself together I got down to the work at hand.

Four hours later a knock at my door had me looking up to see James standing there. Are you almost finished he asked?

Give me about ten minutes and I will be.

I've made reservations at Kim's on the Westside of Chicago at noon. He closed the door and I finished my work and met him in the lobby. Putting his hand on the small of my back he guided me outside to a waiting limo. We walked into Kim's and it was the most beautiful restaurant I had ever seen. The ceilings were high and the décor was a decorator's dream. Tables were spaciously sitting in every inch of the main floor. There were four tiers inside all seemed to be bigger than the other. The rooms were surrounded by water that seemed to be coming down the walls. Statues of women and men were positioned all around the room. The biggest bar I had ever seen circled the entire room evolving ever so slightly so that you were never in the same place at any given time. The owner came up as James and I made our way inside and gave James a bear hug. Welcome back to Kim's he said. It's been a long time no?

His thick Spanish was apparent when he spoke. James talked while he led us to a table. After we were seated he sent a waitress over to take care of us. James gave our order and then sat back and looked at me.

I looked over and asked why are you staring at me like that?

You are beautiful but you know that don't you? I didn't say anything so he continued. It's kind of hard for me to say this but I came all the way here to ask for your forgiveness.

I opened my mouth to say something and he held up his hand to stop me. Let me finish. I never loved you and I had no intention of ever marrying you, I'm sorry for that. I won't deny that I should have told you from the beginning but I didn't. I never had any desire other than to take you to bed. I looked at the man who I loved and wanted to throw my water in his face but I contained myself because I wanted to hear everything he said. I'm sorry I used you and when things got too hot I thought up the ideal to send you here. I didn't think that you would move on without causing a scene. I couldn't risk that with my reputation. I'm a changed man from what you knew a year ago.

I came to say I'm sorry. I'll pay for your moving cost and clear everything up here and you can come back to Florida. I looked at him with so much hatred and contempt in my heart that I wanted to jump across the table and strangle him. He waited for me to say something and when I didn't he said can you forgive me?

I got up from the table and moved as if in slow motion towards the entrance outside I hailed a cab and gave my address. I couldn't think I could barely breathe. Once inside my home I drank a whole bottle of wine and I still didn't feel anything I was numb. I couldn't even think. My cell was ringing none stop and I couldn't bring myself to look at it.

I got up went into the kitchen and found another bottle and went back and sat down on the couch and opened it pouring another drink that's when I broke down and cried. I cried for an hour not even hearing my door bell or my phone my heart was broken all I heard was that voice in my head saying fool, fool, and fool. What a big fool I was to choose a man over my family. How can I go back home and face my family? My mom thought I was getting married and she thought everything was going great in my life but my life was turned upside down. I could just see James and Jim having a big ole laugh at my expense. I got mad then and I wanted both of them to hurt like I was hurting. Jim was not as careful as he thought he had been and I had uncovered some damaging information on him a while back. I could destroy his career and bring down his company if I chose too. And that company was co-owned by James.

As the wheel turned in my head I finished the second bottle of wine and made my way back into the kitchen for another bottle. I cried and drank some more. He never loved me, he had used me, and now he wanted to make amends and throw me aside like a dirty dish rag. Oh no, it was not going down like that. I cried some more and finished off the third bottle of wine. I wanted to hit something or better yet someone. I cried some more. I didn't have any friends because I didn't want anyone in my business so I couldn't call anyone and talk and then I thought about GG yeah GG would talk to me and give me some good advice.

The phone rang two times before a small voice said hello. GG this is Rebecca and then I lost it I don't know what all I said because I was crying and talking at the same time.

GG said, "Hush baby God is going to work it all out now let me talk. You left God He never left you. He's been protecting you and you haven't been grateful."

Did you actually think that trouble was not going to find you? As GG talked I was sobering up fast. God had a plan for you even before you were formed in your mother's womb. When you met that man you had already perceived the outcome in your mind differently. You thought he was your husband and you started giving him privileges he didn't deserve. You didn't talk to God about him now he's showing you his true colors. You were so busy pleasing him and doing things that you missed the process that got you where you are today. Now acknowledge what you have to do, it was nobody's fault but your own. Own up to your mistakes and move forward. Your mind should have gone beyond your needs a long time ago, don't get offended because you thought you knew him he just did what you allowed him too.

The same God you left in Florida is the same God in Chicago. Be happy about your life, happy that you know the truth. Have a heart of gratitude, because he was only standing in the way of your destiny. You will get through this not because you are strong but because God is. When GG stopped talking my tears had dried up and I was ready for battle. Not the kind that would wound but the kind that would heal. I talked to her for a while longer hung up took a hot shower and lay down for a while. I must have dosed off because when I woke James was at my door shouting my name. Opening the door I asked him what now?

You didn't think you hurt me enough? He dropped his head and asked if he could come in, I moved back and he entered.

Look Rebecca I'm not the same man you left in Florida I'm changing because I need too if I hurt you I'm sorry. I just want to be right moving forward in what I'm trying to do. I've hurt a lot of women and now I'm doing a lot of apologizing and I'm trying to right what I did wrong. I never promised marriage I knew you were thinking marriage I just said that I would stay in Florida and sell everything before I joined you. Truth is my life changed and I want to right those I did wrong. Please tell me you forgive me. I thought about what GG said and I said I'm trying you have caused me a whole lot of pain and I want to kill you right now but you have to give me some time to think about everything you've said now go before I change my mind and do what I want to do. After he left I cried my last tear and went to bed.

Next morning I went to work talked to Jim and explained that I was leaving and packed my desk. Jim asked questions that I didn't answer and I walked out. Home I was going home and I was getting my life back.

Jim was devastated. He had no idea what had just happened or what was fixing to happen. He walked to his office concerned that his life as he knew it was about to come crashing in. He started going through books and he called his accountant to make sure everything was in order. He knew that things were about to change for the worst the feeling would not go away and an air of dread hung with him as he checked and rechecked his numbers. He stayed late that night shredding anything that he thought would point back to him.

What a lousy time for James to come. Did he already know or was he just sniffing around trying to find something. He always had a knack for smelling out trouble in his businesses. When he had done all he thought he could possibly do he got up put his jacket on and went home.

Chapter 6 – DEAD or ALIVE

Knowledge is power. That's what James had heard all of his life. Something didn't sit right with his spirit when he talked with Jim about the cases and the office. Wisdom told him something was not right at the firm. His works told him to go check things out. He was restless, and his gut told him it had nothing to do with Rebecca but everything to do with Jim. He couldn't sleep. He asked his driver to take him back downtown to his office. He got out and headed for the side entrance where he knew his key fit. He stopped short when he heard footsteps behind him. He had trained with the best during his years in the army; nothing took him by surprise.

As he turned to his left, something hit him hard on his right side knocking the wind of him. James was down before he knew what hit him. Rebecca had not heard anything else from James. At one point during the night, she decided to take him up on his offer to transfer her back to Florida with all expenses paid. She thought that only fair. Tossing and turning, she thought about what GG said and knew that GG was right. Rebecca thought about her mom and her family that she had left behind. She knew that it was time to return home. Someone had once said that home was where the heart was. Rebecca knew better though. She knew that her heart was with James. Maybe one day he would realize that and want her as much as she wanted him.

She wondered if she would ever stop loving him. She waited until daylight to call James to except his offer. The call went directly to voice mail. She waited another hour and tried him at Jim's office. She called the main line at the office and got a voice recording, which was strange. She waited a full ten minutes to call Jim again because he always came in at seven sharp. Ten minutes after seven Rebecca tried Jim's office; Jim answered himself, which was odd.

"Jim, why are you answering the phone?"

"My secretary hasn't showed up this morning, and I thought it was her that was calling.

Is there something I can help you with?" "Have you heard from James this morning? I have been trying to reach him all night, and I keep getting his voice mail. I find that strange because he always answers when I call."

"The last time I talked to him was right after you left yesterday. Did you change your mind about staying?"

"No, I didn't and I pray for your sake that you tell him what you have been up to with the company." I heard a click and the line went dead. I thought to myself. "That low down dog thinks he's going to get away with doing dirt with the company. It will never work. Everything has a way of coming back on you. I know I'm a living testimony." I called my mom and told her I was coming home soon. She cried. I knew she would. Although we didn't see eye to eye about things, I always knew that she loved me, and I loved her. The day was halfway over, and I still heard no word from James. I began to worry. At two, I tried Jim's office again. I was relieved when his secretary answered the phone. Sandra and I went way back we would often share our secrets with each other.

"Hey, it's me Rebecca. Is Jim out of his meeting with James yet?"

"James never showed up, and Jim is anxious about something. He keeps asking every fifteen minutes if I have heard anything from James. and the answer is still no." "Are you telling me James didn't call or show up this morning?"

"Yes, that's what I'm saying."

"That's not like him he would have called one of us by now. Would you check and see if he took a flight out today and get back with me?"

"Sure, I'll call you back within the hour." I couldn't imagine James just running off without saying anything to anyone, but once a snake always a snake. Still, I had a sinking feeling in the pit of my stomach, and it wouldn't go away. I paced the room and tried calling James again; I really needed him to help with the expenses of getting me back to Florida. Again, his cell went straight to voice mail. While I was pacing at home, Jim was getting concerned that his partner was talking to the police about his activities. He knew that when it came to running a tight ship, James was the master. He called his accountant again just to make sure his paper work added up with the fiscal year. He didn't want any numbers off. Jim knew that when it came down to it, James would have him arrested without even blinking an eye. The only thing he could do now was wait.

James secretary, Mrs. Pittman, had been calling him on and off since he had called yesterday asking her to look into a couple of cases. Jim had told him that he didn't accept the cases, but court records showed that he not only accepted them, he had won a hefty settlement. She was getting worried that he had not called back, and now, his voicemail was full. Something was wrong she just knew it. She could not stand it another second so she called Rebecca. Rebecca was the only other person whom she knew she could trust in that law firm. Thinking back to when she first met Jim Davis, she knew that he was fake and a snake. Nonetheless, no amount of talking to James would make him think less of Jim.

James would only laugh when she called Jim a snake. "Now Bea," James would say. "You can't go around judging people. What if he talked bad about you? What would you think if I told you he thought that you were a prison warden, always guarding me and not letting anyone approach me?"

"I would say that he's absolutely right. Why did you choose him to partner up with anyway?" "It's a long story and maybe one day I'll tell you if you're nice to him." "Humph," was all he heard as I left the room.

I checked his flight schedule first and found that he had neither booked another flight home nor had he flown home this morning. Next I dialed Rebecca number, and she answered on the first ring. "Thank God you're safe," she said when I answered. "I've been calling you all day." "Rebecca. this is Bea. I was calling you because I haven't heard from James since yesterday, and I thought that you had talked to him or seen him at the Chicago office." "I'm going crazy because he was paying for my return trip home and was shipping all my things back there. I haven't seen him or spoken to him since yesterday. Something is wrong; I'm calling the Chicago Police now."

"Wait don't do anything until I hear from Mrs. Connor."

"Who is that?" "She is Jim's secretary."

"Oh, I call her Sandra. I already talked to her, and she doesn't know any more than we do. I'm waiting to see if James took any flights anywhere." "I looked into that before I called you, and he didn't. I'm hanging up now; I'm reporting him missing."

"Missing?" I hung up and sat down thinking, "James missing?" "No, I didn't think so I was thinking that he dodged me and made me look like a fool again." Thinking that something had actually happened to him was unimaginable. I called Jim again and got his voice mail. "What was going on with these two? A storm was coming and I didn't even see it."

Jim sat in his office wondering what James was doing. He decided to try his cell one more time before he left for the day. No answer and he couldn't leave a message either. He slowly got up and put on his jacket. He told his secretary he was leaving for the day and walked toward the elevators. Just as he pushed the buttons, the doors opened, and two detectives got out. Looking him dead in the eye, one of them asked if he was Jim Davis. He tried not to appear nervous.

He answered, "Yes, can I help you?"

The taller one pulled his badge out and said, "I'm Detective Steve Langford and this is Detective Reese. We would like to speak to you in private if you have a second."

Jim said, "Yes, of course," and led them to his office telling Mrs. Pittman to hold all calls. As soon as he shut the doors he asked them, "What is this about?"

"We got a call from someone in Florida who was concerned about a Mr. James Favors. Do you know him?"

"Yes, he's my business partner."

"When was the last time you talked to him?"

"We talked yesterday, and we were supposed to meet this morning, but he never showed up. I have been trying to reach him all day."

"Do you think it strange that he won't answer?"

"Sure I do, but he's a busy man." "Tell us how you know him." "We went to college together. After college, he went down south, and I stayed here. About ten years ago, he opened up his first law firm in Florida. He called me to see if I would be interested in being his partner. I didn't want to move south so he opened up this firm here in Chicago. I head this firm, and he heads the one in Florida."

"Is that right," Detective Reese asked.

"Yes, that's right," I replied. I disliked him instantaneously.

"Do you mind if we take a look around?"

"No, go right ahead." As they looked from room to room I tried to remain calm, but my insides were shaking so badly. I had never come in contact with detectives before, and they scared me. I looked out and noticed that the tall one was talking to Mrs. Pittman. She seemed very nervous. I had to get myself together. When they came back into my office, Detective Langford informed me that I needed to be available for questioning in the future. They told me not to take a flight or anything. On their way out, they took a look around the garage area. I waited until the elevator door closed before I let out my breath and began to breathe normally again. I called Mrs. Connor into my office and asked her what was said to her.

"They only asked about Mr. James. They wanted to know when the last time he was here and the last time I talked to him."

"Is that all they asked?" "Yes that's all." We both left the office at the same time. During the elevator ride to the garage, we both were lost in our own thoughts. I was thinking about the dirt I had done that was quickly catching up with me. As I walked to my car, I saw that the detectives were still looking around. Detective Langford was getting ready to call it a night when he noticed something shiny laying close to the side entrance to the building. Walking toward the object he saw that someone had dropped a cell phone. He picked it up and opened it.

He discovered that it belonged to James Favors. He called his partner over and they quickly closed off that section of the garage. They called headquarters to send out the special squad. He knew that the sooner they act on a missing person case the fresher the clues were. Detective Reese had already made calls to check out what kind of man James was. He also looked into James's spending habits. They had two detectives were in route to Florida to talk to anyone that knew James. James's disappearance happened on Langford's beat.

He took it personally and would leave no stone unturned. No one just came to his city and disappeared; he had a ninety-nine percent crime solving rate under his belt. He knew in his gut that he would keep that record. He left everyone at the scene and drove to the hotel where James had been staying. At the desk he showed his badge and asked the clerk, "Has Mr. Favors checked out?"

"No sir, his credit card is still on file and active."

"I need you to show me his room." He followed the clerk up to the room and looked around. He paused in the middle of the room. Many didn't know that Steve Langford believed in God, and He was the key to his success. As he stood praying silently to God, he had a thought, and he decided to follow up on it. He thanked the clerk and left. As he drove through his city, he thought himself, "I'm the luckiest man alive. I have a beautiful wife who had encouraged me to seek God early in our relationship and I had. I love her more than she would ever know." Back at the office he made a few calls. He finally called it a night. He knew that tomorrow would be a busy day.

Jim had already made several calls, and he was running scared. He was on his third drink when the doorbell chimed. He looked out the side curtain and wondered why she was at his door. Opening the door was the biggest mistake he could have made; it was the last thing he remembered. She had to work quickly. Things were getting out of hand. She knew that Jim was a snake, and he had to be eliminated.

He was one of the reasons that her life was so messed up. He had promised her that he would help her, and he had broken that promise years ago. She called her friend from the truck and together they carried Jim's limp body to the truck. She looked around and made sure she left nothing out of place. About two years ago she had come across some property on the back side of the city and had purchased it.

"What are we going to do with him," her friend asked breaking into her thoughts.

"Take him to the cabin; by then, I will have figured out what to do. He has been a thorn in my side for years. Now it's payback time."

"You are still giving me what you promised me right?"

"Yes, you know that I could not have pulled this off without you. Thanks to Jim, I lost everything. He got wealthier and wealthier where as I got empty promises." After pulling up to the cabin, they lifted Jim out the truck, carried him inside, tied him up, gagged him, and waited for him to come around. Her friend got them drinks, and they waited. Jim was trying to open his eyes. When he finally did, he saw his worst nightmare staring at him. He tried to move, but he was tied down with something. She approached him and just smiled. Jim started talking so quickly; she held up her hand. "An empty promise is all you made. You had me believe you, and you were full of lies. Today is the day that all this ends."

Jim looked into her eyes and knew that nothing he could say would make things better. When he had composed himself enough to try and talk to her, a man whom he had seen before walked into the room. Jim recognized him and tried to reason with him. "We are done talking the man informed him. I need you to take care of a few details, and I need them done now."

Chapter 7 – Missing Pieces

Detective Langford touched down in Florida. After retrieving his bags, he went to pick the rental car up. While waiting for the car, he searched his phone for messages. He had everything he needed. Once he left the airport, he headed to the hotel to freshen up. He needed to pay Pastor Ron a visit. He could feel the tension falling off the closer he got to the hotel. While showering, he talked to God. "Lord, I know that You wouldn't bring me this far to leave me. I know that You always have a good plan for my life. As I do Your will, You will bring my plans into action and see that they line up with Your will. Then, I know that they will be successful. I thank You now, and I will always be grateful to You." He stepped out the shower, picked up his phone, and got directions to Pastor Ron's home. He knew that answers would be found there. Then he would be able to piece everything together.

Christine looked out the kitchen window at her husband Her heart was filled with so much love for him. She knew that the agony he was going through was causing him a great deal of pain. He missed James and had begun feeling helpless. She watched him look toward Heaven, close his eyes, and shake his head. She couldn't help either.

The doorbell chimed. She left the window to see who was at the door.

"Yes?" "Hello, my name is Detective Steve Langford," the man stated when she opened the door. After pulling out his badge, he explained his visit. Christine moved aside to let him in. "I hope that I'm not disturbing you, but I would like to speak to Pastor Ron."

Everyone in town had been talking about the disappearance of James. Christine knew that this detective was here for the same reason. She showed him to the backyard where her husband was sitting in the gazebo. Pastor Ron got up and walked toward his wife and the detective. Detective Langford introduced himself, and Pastor Ron told him to take a seat. Pastor Ron asked Christine to bring out lemonade for the two gentlemen.

"I came here to see if you can shed light on James. I was told that you and he are old friends. Whatever you can tell me will go a long way in finding him."

As they talked, Pastor Ron knew in his heart that this man was a child of God. Neither seemed to notice Christine return with the lemonade. Pastor Ron told the detective about how he had met James and explained about their relationship. He also told the detective about the affairs of which he knew. When he finished, the detective had written down everything he thought could be useful in trying to find James. Steve stood, shook hands with Ron, and told him he would be in touch.

As he pulled out the driveway, he looked back and saw Christine hug her husband. Seeing them together reminded him of how much he missed his wife.

Christine came out and wrapped her arms around her husband and reassured him that everything was going to be alright. As they walked back into the house, a car pulled into the driveway. They both looked up and saw Rebecca getting out coming toward them. "What a wonderful surprise," Christine said while giving her a hug. "I didn't know you were home."

"I just got in about an hour ago. I came by to see if you and Pastor had heard the news."

"Come on inside and have a glass of lemonade while we talk," Christine told her. After sitting down at the table, Rebecca began to tell of all the things that had happened to her in Chicago. She began to cry. Pastor Ron started to console her and to tell her that it was alright.

"I made a mess of my life. He told me he loved me, and I thought that when I moved he was going to tie up loose ends and marry me! Now he's missing and is probably dead! He came into the office, took me to lunch, and apologized to me. He told me the truth. He never loved me, and he didn't want to marry me. However, he offered to pay my way back to Florida. I told him to get out. I was so hurt and disappointed. Now he's missing, and all I can think about is the worst."

Fresh tears began to flow. "I wanted him dead because of the way he had treated me."

Christine got up and put her arms around Rebecca. Christine gave her a shoulder on which to cry. Pastor Ron gave her tissues and told her to dry her eyes.

"It's not your fault that he's missing; stop beating yourself up. Everyone will have to give in account for him or herself. Before he left Florida, he told me he was going to apologize to everyone he had deceived. You were first on his list and he did that. Now it's time to pull yourself together. Try to help in any way you can."

"All I know is that Jim was acting kind of strange because he had reason to do so. He had done so many illegal things in the firm, and he knew that James was on to him. When I left the firm yesterday, I brought papers with me that he thought were destroyed. I have proof that he was padding the books and hiding money in different accounts."

Pastor Ron said, "You have to call the detective with that information every bit helps in an investigation. I'll call him for you, and you can tell him everything you know."

After Pastor left the room, Rebecca looked at Christine. "Do you think that this information I have will be helpful?" "Anything you have will help." The two women talked a while longer. Pastor came back in the room told Rebecca that Detective Langford would meet her at her mom's house around six that evening.

After Rebecca left, the two sat outside on the porch talking about the events that had taken place that day. "Honey, are you thinking the worst, or are you thinking that God will work things out?"

"I think God has a purpose and a plan for each of us. He will provide for us and take care of us. God has a plan for James's life, and I don't think that He is finished yet."

"So, you think James is still alive?"

"Let's just pray that God is still in the blessing business."

When Steve looked at the next name on his list, he wouldn't let himself believe that it was the same person he had dated all those years ago. He was so surprised that her name was among the people on his list. After ringing the doorbell, he straightened his tie for the third time before she opened the door. When he looked at her all of the memories came flooding back.

"Hi," he said.

Shree looked at the tall man standing in her doorway, and her mouth fell open.

Oh my goodness, Steve, I have been thinking about you, and here you are standing at my door! Unbelievable! What are you doing here? How did you find me?"

So many questions came out that Steve began to laugh.

"I'm sorry; come on inside. I must look crazy asking so many questions. While stepping inside, he looked around at her home and was impressed. "You have a beautiful home," he said. "You did well. I always hoped you would."

Shree smiled at him. "I wanted to thank you for pushing me out of your nest and making me stand on my own two feet, but I couldn't find a phone number or an address for you. And now here you are."

"Let me formally introduce myself to you. Hi I'm Detective Steve Langford." Again Shree's mouth fell open and she said, "You are the detective that I'm waiting for?" She started to laugh. "You? A detective? Wow! I would never have thought you had it in you." They both laughed, and she said, "Sit, let me get you something to drink.

While walking into the kitchen, she thought about how far they both had come. After pouring lemonade into glasses, Shree went back into the den shaking her head. As she was walking toward him, Steve noticed the baby bump under Shree's sundress and wondered if there was a husband somewhere. "So I see congratulations are in order," Steve said. "What?" She asked looking confused. "On the baby," Steve said. Oh thank you, I didn't think it showed. After she sat down, Steve asked her if she was married.

"No, this happened before the marriage."

"So you are engaged?"

"No before the engagement. It's a long story, and you didn't come here to hear this one I know. So you are the detective working on James's case?"

"Yes, and I was hoping you could shed some light on this situation. Can you tell me about him?"

"I know that he's an attorney. He owns one of the largest law firms in Florida. He's a deacon at Mt. Nebo Church, and he's my baby father," I said while rubbing my stomach. "We started seeing each other about a year ago, not in a relationship, but I thought it was heading there. He would invite me out to dinner or lunch. We would go to concerts or plays, and I was really falling for him. I thought the feeling was mutual. A couple of months ago I found out I was pregnant. Then, I found out that I wasn't the only woman he was seeing. Of course, I was devastated. He came over after church a couple of Sundays ago. He was thinking that we would have dinner and maybe something else. I gave him a check for everything he had done for me. Of course, that didn't go well, and I put him out. That night I went to my grandmother's house. When I got back, he was sitting in my driveway. I asked him to leave."

"Wait a minute, what grandmother? I thought your family was deceased."

"On no, she's not my biological grandmother. She's just a great woman I met when I first got here. Everyone calls her GG. She's been like my grandmother and more; she's family to me." "I understand go on."

"He was upset when he left here. That night I really was going to tell him about the baby, but after we started talking, I got so angry with him. I gave him a check and put him out. Steve, if something has happened to him, I don't know what I will do. He is a good man, and after I talked to GG, I was going to tell him. I swear I was."

"I believe you. You said that you found out he was talking to other women. Can you remember their names?" Shree gave him the names. Afterward, they both sat in silence for a while.

"Did you ever marry," Shree asked. "Yes, I met her when I was in training. She was the sister of one of the guys there. On graduation day, she walked in, and I couldn't take my eyes off her. That night I asked her out, and we've been together since. Her name is Erika. She's stood by my side pushing me and sometimes pulling me to be the man that God ordained me to be. Without her, I don't know where I would be. I've been on this job, and it's been hard. But it's my destiny you know what I mean? I feel whole. One day I would like you and James to meet her."

"Wait a minute you just said James do you know something I don't?" "No, but I know that my gut tells me he's still alive, and when that happens, my instincts are not wrong. I don't want you to worry, but if you think of anything else let me know."

Christine was in the kitchen cooking a light meal when the phone rang; the caller ID said it was Nicki. "Hey baby, is everything alright?

Yes mom, I have been thinking about some of the women in my women's group who dated James. There is something about one of them that I remember was kind of strange when I talked with her one on one. Maybe it's nothing, but the minute she said it, she denied she was talking about the same guy. I had forgotten about it until tonight so I wanted to call you to see what you think."

"Go on," Christine said. "I have one on one's with every woman that joins the Women Ministry Group. I give each woman something that she can relate to in our meetings. You remember Mary Ann. She's the woman in the choir that does most of the leading. She and I were talking about her family, and she mentioned that she had a step-brother who was sending her money every month. However, he had stopped, and she was having a hard time financially. He had stopped answering her calls. She said he lived in Chicago, his name was Jim, and he owned a law firm.

I asked her if he was the same Jim that James was partners with; she freaked out and said she didn't say Jim. She said his name was Franklin and I know I heard Jim. After that, she refused to talk about her step-brother so I let it go. Do you think that detective could use this information?"

"I think that he could; let me call Ron, and you can run it by him." While mom went to get him on the phone I began to have doubts about telling the story again. Maybe I was crossing the line of being a pastor's wife by revealing information that members gave me. Pastor came on the line as soon as I had that thought.

"Hey Nicki, how are you? Your mama tells me you have some information that might be useful."

My tongue was glued to the roof of my mouth; I didn't know what to do. He paused in mid-sentence and said, "It's alright baby girl; I know that you're battling within yourself. Sometimes information shared is not always used, but it may be helpful in saving a life."

I took a deep breath and repeated what had been told to me. I was wishing to God that I was doing the right thing. After I had finished, Pastor said I had done the right thing, and he would pass the information on to the detective. I felt kind of relieved that I wouldn't have to talk with him. I hated this sort of thing.

Chapter 8 – Stolen Identity

Detective Langford pulled up at Rebecca's mom house at six sharp. While sitting in the car, he looked around the neighborhood that her mom lived in and thought about his upbringing and his old neighborhood. His cell rang before he could go back down memory lane. It was Pastor Ron. After receiving the information, he got out the car and knocked on the door. Rebecca answered the door and invited him inside. He admired the way her mom had furnished the home. "You know this home looks a lot like the home I came from."

"Really," Rebecca said. "My mom works as a store manager, and while I was away, I tried to make her life a little easier by sending money home."

"I understand; my mom died a few years ago. But that's not why I came, can you tell me about Jim?"

When Rebecca finished the story, Steve had an idea of where he was going next. He thanked her and told her to give him a call if she thought of anything else. Rebecca walked him out. She sat on the porch swing thinking about how she was going to make her life meaningful after the disaster she had made of it so far. She began to pray.

"Lord, I'm speaking over my situation today. I know that I haven't been all that You planned me to be, and I'm sorry. Forgive me for straying when You needed me to stand still. Forgive me of my sins, and let them be remembered no more. Lord, allow me to make things right with You. Lead me back to Your path of righteousness, and Lord, please give me a second chance to make things right. This is my prayer in the powerful name of Jesus Christ. Amen."

She continued to swing back and forth until she felt calm. A car door closed, and she opened her eyes to see her mom stepped out of the car. She looked tired. After getting up to give her mom a hug, she said, "I'm so sorry I left when you needed me the most. Please forgive me mom. I'm going to make it up to you."

Her mom hugged her tighter and said, "You already have; let's go inside and have dinner."

Sitting at the kitchen table with her mom was priceless, and Rebecca knew it. You know mom, sometimes we forget that moms always know what's best for us. I fought you so hard in my sin, and you still prayed for me.

I'm grateful for a mom like you. You were right all along. You tried to tell me that James didn't love me, and I just wouldn't listen. Thank you for your continual prayer. I ran off as quickly as I could from you, and look how God brought me back to the same place from which I was running. Nothing came together as I had imagined it would. I wanted to get away from here just to show people that I could be successful. I came back with what I left with; how's that for successful?"

Mom looked at me and said, "The work of the Devil will not win against God. Those who walk with God find true shelter and protection in Him. I'm not happy that you went through what you did, but I am happy that God kept you through it all. I'm glad that you're home and that you realize we are nothing without God. Baby, God has a purpose and a plan for all of our lives. Now you've given up your usual so God can move into the unusual. You're gaining more clarity, and now you can move forward in the right direction. The most beautiful people I know are the ones who have known defeat, suffering, struggling, and loss. There is beauty in the ones who have found their way out of those depths. So as you sit here tonight pouring out your bitterness, God is pouring out His peace into your life. Now the new beginnings are coming."

She patted my knee, got up, and said, "I'm going to shower, watch a little TV, and go to bed." I stood up, kissed her, and watched her go inside. My mom was one strong lady.

When Steve got to the next house he decided to just sit in the car and watch to see if anything unusual happened. The grass was rather high and needed cutting. There was a light on in the house, and he could see movements from the shadows. A blue van pulled up, and his instincts kicked in. He knew he had his first real lead since he left Chicago. While following the van from a safe distance, he checked in with his partner to bring him up to speed on what was going on. He felt began and finally started to relax. The van pulled up at an ATM machine on Collins Avenue, an upscale mall in Miami. The driver got out of the car.

I had my camera ready; I took about five good shots of him from different angles. He got back in the van, and I continued to follow them around the Miami area. Next, they stopped at Aventura Mall. This mall was popular because it was three stories and was filled with designer shops. They both got out, and I found a good spot to wait while they went inside. Almost two hours went by before they finished shopping. Both had way too many bags to carry. I watched them load the bags into the van, and this time the woman did the driving. I was slightly confused when they headed back northwest, but I trailed them to their next destination. It turned out to be a car dealership, Mercedes-Benz to be exact. They both went inside the dealership; I was praying that I wouldn't lose this interesting couple. My phone went off and my partner informed me who the guy was.

He had just finished a doing time in Florida State Prison-East, the largest prison in Florida.

"Well this is interesting," I said to Andy, my partner. "See if he had any visitors while he was there."

Ok Steve, I'll get right back to you, and hey, don't do anything that puts you in danger."

"You know me man, I go strictly by the books." I watched the salesman come out, look at the old van, shake his head, and go back inside. An hour went by; Andy called back and gave me information on his only visitor in ten years. "She showed up around a year ago and had made visits once a month for the last year."

"Got you," I said to myself. Now everything was beginning to make sense, but I was still puzzled about a few things. Anyway, like my wife would say, "It would all come out in the wash."

Finally, they came out and looked around the lot. I saw them get inside a brand new baby blue Mercedes S-Class Sedan. "They liked the color blue," I thought. His phone rang; he answered and chatted a few minutes keeping his eyes on the car praying that they would only drive one off the lot. She came out first. She had the biggest grin on her face; he walked out next grinning likewise. They appeared to be arguing once they reached the car. She seemed to be winning because she got in the driver's seat and he in the passenger side. I started my car and wondered where they were headed now.

Tina Melson

I called Andy back with the information I had received from the phone call; he went to work promising me he'd have the answers soon.

"I really think we're spending too much money," he said as I slid behind the most beautiful car I had ever possessed.

"You are not going to spoil this for me," I said, parking beside the old beat up van. I got out to retrieve our new clothes and shoes. "We have never been able to afford any of these things, and I will not let you ruin my happiness."

"I'm not trying to ruin anything I just don't want to go back to that hell hole I was in. I was so nervous when that guy ran my license and credit card; what if something had gone wrong in there, what would you have done?" "Nothing happened so why are you complaining; we got the best of the best. Let's go find a hotel and finish up this party!" I was on top of the world. Nothing and no one were going to ruin this for me.

"Do you really think no one is going to look for him," he asked breaking into my thoughts.

"Who's going to miss him," I asked. "Stop worrying about it. You wanted the good life. Now just live it," I told him smiling my best smile. He smiled back, and we headed out the car lot. Neither of us looked back. If we had, we would have seen a car pull out behind us. We pulled up to the Breakwater South Beach Hotel. I couldn't believe how nice it really was. The valet parked our car after we got our shopping bags and luggage.

The staff came and took our things as we walked into the hotel. After getting the suite, we were led to the most beautiful suite I had ever seen. The two thousand square foot suite had two bedrooms, two kitchens, two and a half bathrooms, three balconies and a living room bigger than my rental house. My mouth hung open at the sight of such beauty. He closed the door and said, "I'm hungry. Let's change, and go find some food."

"I'll shower and change in the bedroom over there, and you can take the other one."

"Wait a minute, we are not sleeping in separate bedrooms after all I've done," he said giving me an angry look.

"No, I just mean we can get ready quicker if we use both rooms." The answer satisfied him, and he disappeared into the other bedroom.

Steve knew that they were settled in for the night, and he knew he had to leave them. First, he had to call and secure back up for the night before he could leave; he didn't want those two getting away.

Chapter 9 – Cold Blood Killer

He wondered if someone would find him. He had been in this small room long enough. He couldn't get the rope to budge. It was tied so tightly around his body. He'd been trying everything to get free to no avail. "What was the story with these people? What did they want from him?" He'd offered them everything he could think of, and they wouldn't budge. "What did they want?" If he could only get his hands untied. He continued to look around to see if there was anything he could use to get loose.

"Think," he said to himself. "Think!"

If they wanted him dead, he would already be. He had apologized to the woman and had pled with her. She had only slapped him in his face. He deserved that he supposed. Then, she left, and he hadn't seen her since. The three clowns that had manhandled him were strong; he was outnumbered. He had fought with everything in him, but it had not been enough. He was in a room with no windows; he was tied down like a hog. He had nothing else to do but think. He thought about Rebecca and wondered if she had made it back to Florida.

He wondered if she had told anyone what she thought he was up to, or was she still working in the office? He knew that she was going to talk eventually. "Would he be there to explain himself?" Lord, he hoped so.

The policeman assigned to the two watched them as they headed down to the dining area. Although they seemed to enjoy each other's company, he thought them an odd couple. She looked to be a lot older than her gentlemen friend. When they finished, he watched as the man took out a wallet. He went through a number of cards before choosing one. After the bill had been paid, they walked outside, and the detective followed at a safe distance. They entered a club that was in full swing. He made his way inside and sat at the bar so he could keep an eye on them. They spent way too much money and seemed not to have a care in the world.

 Now he was curious; he wondered where the guy worked. The man was spending money like he owned several companies, but he looked too young and inexperienced to have a company. Besides, you just didn't blow money like water. He watched as they danced and had way too much to drink. About two hours later, they were finally ready to go. He followed them back to the hotel and watched them take the elevator up to their suite. He made himself comfortable in a large chair in the lobby where he could see every entrance. He began to read the novel he had brought with him.

After a while, the bellboy came over and started a conversation with him; the officer had been on watch there before so the staff knew him.

"Did you see the couple that got on the elevator just now," he asked me.

"As a matter of fact I did. Do you know them?" I have never seen them before. However, I do know that the card he used and the ID he used have his face on them, but he's not the person to whom the card belongs. I thought about what he said, and I was interested to know more.

I replied, "How do you know that?" "I know the guy who owns the card, and that's not him. He's been in this hotel several times, and that guy is not who he says he is. I don't care what his identification says."

"Really? That's interesting. What does the guy look like?" "He's taller and older than him. He always wears a suit and tie, and he has never gotten drunk or loud. I don't know who that guy is, but I know that man is not Jim Davis." We talked a little more before he was called away. With the information I received, I reported it to Steve immediately. Meanwhile, Shree woke with a start. After realizing she was at home and in bed, she began to pray.

"Lord, You said in Your Word that You would perfect those things pertaining to me. I ask that You protect and keep James safe. Lord forgive me for not telling him about our child. I don't know where he is, but I know that You do. I will rest in the knowledge that You know what is best, not only for me but for James also. I will not fret or give in to worry. I will stay prayerful that You alone will work things out; for I do love You Lord. Amen, Amen and Amen."

Tina Melson

She got out of bed and went to the window.

Shree stared up at the sky and couldn't imagine raising her child alone. She should have done as GG had urged her to and told James that she was carrying his child. She sighed and looked back toward Heaven. She said, "God, please give me a little more time to make it right." After getting back into to bed, she knew it would be a long night. She tossed and turned to make herself comfortable; she thought that James had to be alright. Finally Shree gave up and went downstairs to get a drink of water. She glanced at the clock on the wall; it read three a.m. She dared not call and wake GG; she didn't want her to worry. She decided to call Steve instead. He answered on the first ring. "I hope I didn't wake you. I couldn't sleep."

"No I just got off the phone. Is everything okay?"

"Yes, I was wondering if you had heard anything more about James."

"No, I'm sorry, but don't worry we are working on solving this case."

"What if something bad has happened to James; he's the father of my child." "I know, but don't worry. Everything will be alright."

"What if you never find him; my child will never know his father." "I can only tell you to pray; you know God is able to do exceedingly, abundantly more than we could ever ask of Him. My wife reminds me of this every day." "Tell me about her." He smiled and when he described her to Shree; she could hear the love in his voice. "She keeps me on my toes." "Why haven't you had children?" "Well that's another story. Actually, we're still trying." An hour had gone by so I thanked him for keeping me company and hung up. I felt so much better after talking to Steve; I went back to bed smiling.

Steve made a promise to himself. After talking to Shree, he decided he was going to do everything in his power to find James. As he was leaving the hotel, he checked all his messages. He knew that if he didn't move now it would be too late. He called in the local police department to put them on alert; he then headed to the judge's office to pick up the warrant. When he got to the hotel, everyone was in place. He and a few more officers spoke in the hotel lobby before going up to the room. The manager had given them the keys to the suite, and now he was ready to move.

As he unlocked the door, he heard snoring coming from the room on the left. He pointed to that room and officers slowly moved in that direction. Then he pointed to the bedroom on the right, and he and several officers moved right. As the officers were bringing the man out of the one room, Steve came out of the other room with the woman in cuffs. Gut instinct told him that both rooms would be occupied.

The man began to curse at the woman. He swore that this would happen because she was spending too much money. She, in turn, was yelling at him to be quiet. As we were taking them out the hotel, I saw the bellboy shaking his head. I motioned for the officers to take them outside; I wanted to speak to the bellboy. When I approached him, he began to tell me what he had told the officer last night. Things just clicked in place now the investigation was moving forward.

I contacted Detective Reese to see how far he had gotten, and he informed me of a cabin that was owned by Jim in Dade County, Florida. He also told me that a Mary Ann Kennedy was listed as a tenant. I informed him we had just arrested a Mary Ann Davis whom I suspected was the same woman. I asked him to fly down because I knew that he would be able to help me more here than there. I didn't want to talk to the suspects until he got here. He caught a flight right away.

In the time it would take me to get to the airport, he would be touching down. His flight arrived on time; before I could park and get out, he was walking out the terminal. We shook hands and got in the car.

"Man, I have a hunch that that cabin will turn up something so I'm sending you to Dade County with some local policemen. While you're there, I'll question Mr. and Mrs. Davis."

"Who," Reese asked with a smirk on his face.

"Yeah right," I replied.

I had a look of determination. We walked down the halls of the station, gathered in one of the rooms, and began to strategize our next move. After Reese and the others left, I walked into the interrogation room to face Mr. Jim Davis aka Randall Sanders. "Mr. Davis, you've been a busy man." He looked scared, and I knew he was going to break easily. "Before we get started, let me turn on this recorder." As I reached to turn on the recorder, he began to sweat. "My name is Detective Steve Langford." I began to read him his rights just in case nobody else had. When I finished, I told him that I was waiting for his prints to come back. He immediately confessed that his real name was Randall Sanders.

"Got you!" I thought in my mind. "Would you like to write a statement now? Do you want to make it harder for yourself," I asked pushing a pad and pen toward him.

"If I write a statement, what kind of deal will you give me," he asked. "Listen," I said I don't make deals with criminals "However, for your cooperation we can work something out."

The chief came in and gave me his report. As I read it, I kept looking at the guy sitting in front of me. I was thinking that if they had harmed James, Randall would surely be going away for the rest of his life. The chief motioned for me to step out, and we stepped out into the hallway.

"We found a body in the cabin. They are checking the ID to see who it is." My heart sank. I said a prayer, turned around, and went back in the room. "Mr. Sanders, you are being charged and booked for murder," he looked scared. Then he told the story. "Mary Ann used to visit me when I was in the pen. A couple months before my release, she came to me with this scheme to kidnap her half-brother in Chicago to get money. She knew that he had been embezzling money from the company he worked for so she was sure that she could get him to fly both of us there. Every time she came after that, she had a plan in the works. I was broke. I had nowhere to go, and the things she was telling me sounded good. You know how it is man." I shook my head, and he continued.

"On the day I was released, we drove to her house. She called her brother. During the conversation, there was yelling and screaming from both of them, but in the end, he sent tickets for the both of us.

After we got there, he told her that he was in trouble, and he needed to get out of Chicago. They both put their heads together, and he decided to come back to Florida with us. We flew back. While we were out the next day, she told me her plans to kill him and find someone to alter his ID so I could take on his identity. That wasn't hard because she would have money. That evening during dinner, he told us where his money was and all the things he had done. We all had been drinking, and it was like taking candy from a baby. After he went to bed, I waited until he was asleep. I hit him upside his head, but I swear he wasn't dead. I didn't kill him. I tied him up really good, and we left to get the fake ID's.

When we got back, Mary Ann went in to have a talk with him. I never went back in the room. I don't know what took place in there. She came out looking nervous and said let's go. From then to now, you know the rest."

"I need you to write that down," I said clicking the recorder off.

"Man, I ain't going down for no murder," he hollered as I left the room. I stepped into the room two doors down. She looked unfazed. She didn't look worried or scared so I knew I couldn't play games with her.

Before I could talk to her, the chief came back in the room and motioned me outside into the hallway again. "They've identified the body as Jim Davis. He was shot pointblank in the head." Relief spread through my body, not because Jim had died, but because it wasn't James. I stepped back into the room with the chief beside me. I introduced myself to Mary Ann and read her rights. She asked for a lawyer. "I'm not talking without my lawyer," she informed me.

Chapter 10 – It was all My Fault

GG got a call to go out to lunch. She accepted because she wanted to see what in the Devil she wanted to talk about. Oh, she knew her; that's why GG didn't trust her any further than you could toss a rock. She saw her strutting in the church all dressed up like a peacock wearing those dresses with everything hanging out, shorter than money on payday. Oh yeah, this had to be good; she wasn't going to miss this luncheon. She called Christine to let her know where she would be and with whom.

"Why is she inviting you to lunch?" "I don't know, but it has to be good."

"GG, she never comes near you at church."

"I know that's why it's strange. When she first joined the church, I tried to be kind to her, but she just wouldn't give me a chance. I prayed about it, and God said keep trying. It's been eight years, and I'm still trying."

"Well, maybe God got her attention. That might be why she's offering an olive branch."

"More like an oak tree." "GG, I'm surprised at you!" I said laughing, "You are not being nice."

"I know I just can't figure her out, and every time I talk to God about it, nothing seems to change."

"I'm glad you called so I'll know where you are." "Take your cell phone with you so I can check on you. What time are you meeting her?"

"She said two because she was at work, and it would be a late lunch."

"Do you want me to come?"

"No child, I didn't get this old by being scared to face the Devil and dance with him."

"GG, what am I going to do with you," I said laughing. "I'll be okay I just wanted you to know what's going on." "How well do you know her? You were her first lady." "The conversations I had with her were unsettling. Ron and I prayed with her and things seemed to be better with her, but I don't know. GG, you know I don't like to talk about people, but she went through a rough patch. I suspect that James had a lot to do with it. Now she's in a women's group that Nicki has formed and she attends regularly." "I guess that's all good and everything; maybe it's about the women's group."

"Maybe, I'll call you later. Ron just walked in, and he looks like he needs coffee."

"Okay you know where I'll be."

We hung up, and I busied myself making coffee for Ron. "Was that GG I heard you talking to?" "Yes, and she sends her love.

I wasn't ready to talk about our conversation to Ron just yet." Ron got the paper and began reading so I started breakfast.

Shree was feeling better after her shower. She decided to go in to work for a little while. On the drive there, she thought about the printer that needed to be replaced in her office. She detoured off the main highway and went to Office Deport close by her job. While she was walking through the store looking at all the printers and prices, someone tapped her on the shoulder.

"Hey girl, I thought that was you. How you doing?"

"Good and you? I've been meaning to call you, but time just keeps slipping away."

"How's the pregnancy coming along?" I gave her a strange look and she laughed. "I know James is excited. When are you due?" I mumbled something, and she seemed satisfied.

We stood there for a second until she finally said, "Good seeing you, we need to get together real soon." Then, she walked away. "Was she crazy or just acting like it?" I never told her that I was pregnant let along who the father was. I hardly knew her. I just saw her in church. By the time I left the store, I had worked myself up to being furious. "The nerve of that floozy approaching me like we were friends! Who did she think she was?" I couldn't wait to get to the office and call GG. She was the only one who knew I was pregnant and James was the baby's father.

Not that I tried to hide it, but I had just began to show. Plus, today I had on a big top. I paced the office for another five minutes trying to calm myself down enough to call GG and talk to her calmly. I knew she wouldn't talk to her about me, but right now, I was beside myself. Finally, I picked up the office phone and dialed her number.

"Hello Shree, I was wondering when I would hear from you; you've been quiet through this whole ordeal. Are you okay?"

"I'm good GG. I was calling because something happened this morning, and I thought it was strange."

"What happened? Are you okay?" "You remember the lady at the church who wears all those mini dresses and high heels, but she's older than most? I ran into her at Office Depot this morning, and she acted like we were old friends asking me about the pregnancy and James. I don't even know her; GG, I know you didn't talk to her about me, did you?"

"Child, you know I'm not that type of person. I got a call from her earlier, and she invited me to lunch."

"GG, don't go; she's up to something. I never saw her in that store before today and when I got outside, she had already left. It was as if she followed me there. It was strange. She asked about James. Everyone in Florida knows he's missing. It was kind of scary. What do you know about her?"

"I know that she joined the church about eight years ago. She was married, had two beautiful girls, and wouldn't let me near her. Every time I would approach her, she would go the other way. Two years ago, she stopped bringing the girls to church, and I asked her about it one Sunday, I caught her off guard, and she told me they went to stay with their dad. I didn't have the heart to talk about the affair she had with James so I changed the subject a little."

"Did she touch you? No, nothing like that. I wonder how she knows James is the father."

"I don't know, but if it comes up in our conversation today, I'll let you know."

"No GG, don't go to lunch with her; I don't feel right about this whole thing. I'm going to call Steve and see what he thinks. Don't go out GG, not until I get back with you."

"You know I'm going; she has me curious now."

"GG don't leave until I get back to you."

If you haven't called back by one, I'm calling Uber and I'm meeting her at the restaurant." We hung up, and I called Steve right away. GG was well into her eighties and acted like she was thirty. If something happened to her, I would never forgive myself. My first attempt went straight to voice mail. I left an urgent message. Half hour later I called again, and he picked up. I told him what was going on, and he assured me that he would make sure GG was followed.

He would also run a check on that "floozy" as I called her. I gave him everything I knew about her.

Steve was having a hard time with Mary Ann so he decided to let it rest until they got a lawyer for her. It didn't matter though because he had enough evidence to bury her. She had to confess, and he knew she would. He had to find James; time was running out. He knew that James was in Chicago and had never left. Steve had to wrap up this case and get back there asap. He was trying to piece it together when Shree called. After talking with her, he talked to the captain to make sure someone followed GG around today. He then called Reese so he could follow up with this new information. While he was walking out of the station, he called home; he just wanted to hear her say hello. "Hey baby, how's it going? I can't wait to get back home."

"Hey love, I'm missing you. I can't wait either. You sound tired."

"I am. Do you remember the lady I was telling you about when we met?"

"Are you talking about Shree?"

"Yes, I spoke to her; she's a member of the church where this guy goes. I had to talk to her. I never thought I would see her again."

"Should I be worried?

No, there is no one who can take your place, and you know this." "I love you so much, and I can't wait to get home."

"I can't wait either. Do you have an idea when that will be?"

"I think that I'm going to make it home tonight, if everything goes according to plan."

"Okay, baby, remember that your faith does not stand on the wisdom of man but on the power of God." "Thank you, baby. That's why I love you so much. You always know how to pick me up."

"I'll see you tonight; let me know what time you flight comes in."

"I will. I love you."

"I love you more!" We hung up, and it seemed as if I got more energy than I had in days. One of the detectives came out and told me that Mary Ann wanted to see me again. I went back in to see what she had to say. When I walked in, she was calm unlike the person I had left a few minutes ago. "You wanted to see me?"

"Yes, I want to tell my story."

"The truth I hope," I said to her.

"Yes, the truth." I turned the recorder on and she began.

"My father married Jim's mother when I was three; we did alright growing up. Jim was always the smart one; you already know how he and James became partners. About a year ago, he got into trouble gambling, and he figured out how to embezzle money from the company. He needed me to help him carry out his plans. He flew me to Chicago, and the scheme was carried out. He promised me a big payout that didn't happen. I began to figure out how to get all the money he had hid in various accounts. James showed up in Chicago, and Jim panicked. He called me and decided to fly back here a few days ago. I knew he would go to the cabin so Randall and I made plans to steal the money and take his life. He didn't know that we were coming. We caught him off guard, made him talk, changed IDs, and the rest is history. Yes, I did it. He owed me; he took so much from me and never looked back." When she finished and began to cry, I asked her who shot Him.

"I did. He deserved to die. He was greedy and he didn't care about anyone but himself."

"Where is the gun?" "It's in the hotel room, in the back of the toilet." Dang," I thought we would never have looked there. I looked down at my cell and saw that Reese was calling. "Excuse me for a second I've got to take this," I stepped out the room. That lady you asked me to check out has ties in Chicago; she has a brother there. He was military policeman. He's retired and from my sources, he lost his business a couple months ago so what you want to do?" "Book two flights, call me back, and I'll meet you at the airport.

Shree called GG back and told her to go on but be careful. "I'm always that," was her reply. Uber picked her up at one and dropped her in front of the quiet little Italian Restaurant called Helen's. As she was walking into the building, a waitress greeted her and showed her to a nice table by the window. This way Shree could see her before she came in. "May I get you something to drink," the waitress asked. "Yes dear, bring me a glass of tea while I wait for my friend." She left to get her drink, and GG looked around the restaurant. Not many people were there. She settled in and waited for her to arrive. Her tea arrived and she sipped on it. While looking out the window, GG saw her approaching the door. After the waitress took her drink order, they made small talk. GG knew that she had something on her mind so she waited her out.

"I know that I haven't been very nice to you, but I couldn't talk to anyone else," she said. "I know you see everything, and I know that you are a Godly person. Everybody loves you. I need to get some things off my chest, and I know that you will listen without passing judgment."

"Go on dear," I said "Whatever is bothering you can't be that bad."

"I don't know how bad it is, but I think I need to tell someone."

"Okay," I said "I'm listening."

"Two years ago, I had an affair with Deacon Favors. I'm sure everybody in the church knew. It started out as a one night thing, and it just kept going. I knew that I should have stopped, but I didn't know how to end it. Eventually, it cost me my girls and my husband. I was a housewife, and he worked all the time. Things just got out of hand. I lost it all for a man that didn't love me. When my husband found out, he didn't know who he was, and I never told him. He moved out, got a good lawyer, and took my girls. I thought that James would help me get a lawyer, but he wouldn't help me. He told me that he was not the marrying kind, and he couldn't get caught up in my drama. I couldn't believe it. I got a job, but it didn't pay much. I couldn't fight without money. Every lawyer was so expensive that I had to give up. We went to court. I admitted to the affair, and I lost my girls.

My brother tried to help me get the girls back, but in the process, he lost his business. Now I ruined two people's lives that I loved. I didn't know what else to do. I never told anyone that James was the man. You want to know why not?" I just nodded my head. "Because I ran after him. He didn't pursue me; I pursued him. I would wear tight clothes and high heels and walk right by him. I wanted him to notice. I picked him out. I found out where he lived, and I dropped by his house. He was right; he never pursued me.

Granted, he turned me down at first, but I was persistent.

I found out his favorite places, and I would make myself available. Every time he turned around, he would see me.

I was lonely. I had a good husband just one that was never home. For a whole year I convinced myself and my brother that James was to blame for this mess I had gotten myself into, and now, I have to be real with myself and take the blame for my failed marriage and for what has happened to James." My heart fell when she mentioned James.

"What have you done to him," I asked as calmly as I could.

"I don't know," she said. "I think my brother, Ricky, did something."

"Why would you think that?"

"I told him a week ago that I had overheard someone in the church say that James was in Chicago checking on his company. A few days ago, he told me that he was taking care of everything. After that call, James disappeared and they haven't found him yet. GG, if something has happened I am to blame."

"Hush child, we will sit here until we figure it out. God is a Merciful God, and His grace is sufficient." After a while GG said, "I need to call Pastor Ron."

"Why not Pastor Howard." she asked. "Because Pastor Ron is seasoned if you know what I mean." Pastor Ron pulled up, escorted the two women out to his car, and headed to his home. "GG, I knew something was up with you when Christine didn't say anything about your conversation this morning. Tell me what was so important that I had to drop everything and come get you two."

GG looked at her and told him the story. "What," he said "You have known about this for days and you haven't said a thing?" She nodded and looked out the window. Pastor

Ron hit a button on his phone and relayed word for word what he had been told. Then he hung up and said, "Now we wait."

Chapter 11 – A Fighting Forgiving Chance

The plane touched down and the two of them rushed through the airport to the car that was waiting for them. The drive took forever, but when they arrived it looked like Grand Central Station. It looked like every cop in Chicago was there. He jumped out the car almost before it finished parking and hurried to the house where they were questioning the brother. He wanted to make sure he hadn't missed much. Getting the call from Ron confirmed everything. He crumbled like a piece of dried paper. They found James dehydrated, scratched up, and filthy but otherwise alive. Thank God his sister came forward when she did. The brother told his story. "I lost my business because of him; he destroyed my little sister and her family. I wanted to kill him. He didn't know who I was talking about; he said he would make it right. I just had to tell him who I was talking about so I dragged him to the basement and threw him in that room where you found him. I never went back down to check on him." They placed him under arrest.

The church was full; everyone was dressed in their best. The flowers smelled wonderful. Amanda walked down escorted by Ricky. Next was Nicki escorted by Pastor Howard, and Kim escorted by Reese (yes, the detective). Then the most beautiful bride came in with tears in her eyes. Shree was looking at the most handsome man in the world. James stood up front thanking God for a forgiving and understanding wife. He looked at the first pew, and his throat tightened at the sight of the most beautiful baby sitting in GG's lap. "Thank you, Lord, for giving me a second chance to make things right."

Discussion Questions

Do you think James should have been a deacon? Why or why not?

Why do you think that women are so attractive to men in high places?

If this was happening in your church would you be quiet or would you have to speak up?

About the Author

Author Tina Melson is a mom of four, grandmother of four and great-grandmother of one. After working in the school system for more years than she can count, she wanted to write.

Writing has always been her passion and now that she's retired she has more time to dedicate to the craft.

Tina finds that writing is therapeutic and hopes that her labor of love will not only entertain you but help you find closure to some seasons in your life!

Our God is a God of the unexpected!

The Butterfly Typeface Publishing

The Butterfly Typeface is full service professional writing, editing and publishing company. Our goal is to 'spread the message' of inspiration, imagination and intrigue in all that we do. Whether you hire us to edit, ghostwrite, publish (books & magazines) or web design, you can be guaranteed exemplary customer service, fairness and quality. Our vision, under God's leadership, is to serve and assist in the healing of the heart, mind and soul of *all* people we encounter with integrity, intentional influence and positive purpose.

"We make good GREAT!"

Iris M Williams – Owner
PO Box 56193
Little Rock Arkansas
501.681.0080

www.thebutterflytypeface.com

butterflytypeface.imw@gmail.com